Dedication

To my daughter Bernie, because this book took a lot of work, it was often challenging, and I'm very proud of it. Just like you

BWL Publishing Inc. acknowledges the Government of Canada and the Canada Book Fund for their financial support in creating the Canadian Historical Mysteries.

Funded by the Government of Canada | Canada

BWL Publishing acknowledges the Province of Alberta for their ongoing support through the Alberta Publisher's Cultural Industry Operating Grant.

Alberta Government

Twice Hung

Vanessa C. Hawkins

Print ISBNs
Amazon print 9780228630241
Ingram Spark 9780228630258
Barnes & Noble 9780228630265
BWL Print 9780228630272

Canadian Historical Mysteries

Rum Bullets and Cod Fish - Nova Scotia

Sleuthing the Klondike – Yukon

Who Buried Sarah- New Brunswick

The Flying Dutchman – British Columbia

Bad Omen - Nunavut

Spectral Evidence – Newfoundland

The Seance Murders – Saskatchewan

The Canoe Brigade – Quebec

Discarded – Manitoba

Twice Hung - Prince Edward Island

The Tom Thomson Mysteries – Ontario

Table of Contents

Chapter 1

The day was damp, yet hardly a day at all. Gray clouds hung low in the dismal sky with the promise of reluctant showers. A storm loomed behind the ashen canvass. It had been present ever since the winter months had concluded, and a sodden pall had swept over the coast of the island to remain indefinitely.

Ethel Arsenault longed for the summer days back home at Green's Shore, even though it would be just as wet there. The farmers would prepare their fields, and heave at the heavy earth in hopes it would soon be pregnant with their summer harvest. Ethel liked when the potato fields stood in perfect columns like soldiers. When she was young, she often gathered the flowers in her apron, picking them before they were pruned to make laurels for the boys.

She hadn't done that ever since her brother, Ernest, had moved to Charlottetown to invest in shipbuilding. Now, as the wagon bumped between the muddy ruts of the road, the scent of mussel mud was prevalent over the low-hanging lady slippers and spruce trees that crowded the marshlands. It crept in the nose, more sour than regular fertilizer, and made Ethel and her servant, Beulah, want for warmer weather.

"How much longer till we arrive?" Beulah asked as she rearranged the cushions beneath her bottom. Ethel smiled, sympathetic to her friend's condition. They'd only been traveling a day and had stopped for the night in Cornwall, but even the simple journey in an extravagant stagecoach had taken its toll on their backsides.

"We'll be crossing the Yorke River soon, Miss Murphy," one of the lads called from the front, spitting out a mouthful of chew to plop upon the ground.

"It seems to me like we're headed back in the direction we came, Mr. Carlow!"

Aloysius Carlow—Al—laughed and reached into his pocket to draw out another handful of chewing tobacco. The young man must have taken a liking to Beulah Murphy's robust personality, as he never spoke back to her when she complained or prattled on idly about dirt, mud, flowers, and horses. For a servant, Ethel had to admit that Beulah was unusual, but the girl was cheerful and had a good head on her shoulders, despite her many eccentricities. Ethel loved her dearly.

"Only way to cross the river, Miss, is by Moor's Bridge north of Cornwall. Most people take the boats these days. They tend to be faster."

Mud had speckled the sides of the carriage, but Beulah hung her head out anyway, catching a few freckles upon the slope of her ample cheeks as she peered at the young man's back.

"Never-you-mind about that, Mr. Carlow!"

Al laughed and tugged at the brim of his straw hat that sat low over his brow. "Just sayin' is all, Miss Murphy. Mr. Arsenault would have had you and your lady carried by royalty if you'd have wanted."

Ethel nodded and offered a slight smile in return to Beulah's worried glance. "I'm afraid I'd be bad company for royalty, Mr. Carlow," she said. "Surely the smooth-sailing Princess of Wales would be better suited for someone like my sister-in-law, Dolly."

"She's been carried by it before, no doubt, eh Mr. Humphrey?" Al looked sidelong to include the older gentleman sitting beside him, in the conversation.

Fritz Humphrey, an old friend of Ethel's father, who'd been in the employ of her family for as long as she could remember, grunted. It was the usual response, often muttered around a stalk of wheat or from the neck of a bottle. On the few occasions when Fritz Humphrey did deign a few words, so rare was the occurrence that those around him often listened in marvel of what could have possibly compelled him to speak. This, however, was not one of those times.

Despite Al's nudging, Fritz leant back to drag a pipe from his pocket, proffering the younger man the reins as he went about filling the bowl.

Soon pipe tobacco joined the briny scent of mussel mud. It was a welcome distraction, reminding Ethel of home when both her parents were alive. In the evenings after supper, her father would sit to watch the fields sparkle with fireflies. She wondered if Dolly had such humble memories, or if she'd laugh to hear that some of Ethel's fondest moments were braiding flowers in her brothers' hair and watching bugs alight the sky.

"Are you all right, Miss Ethel?" Beulah's hand was on hers, and it was like fresh warmed bread.

"Just tired. Not used to sitting so long." Ethel smiled and hoped the gesture filled the gauntness of her cheeks. She admired the fullness of Beulah's face, especially when the woman smiled. Though Beulah Murphy was six summers older than Ethel, she carried an air of youth in her features. She was plump, red cheeked and as reliable as a daisy. Ethel was glad to share the journey with her.

"I'd have to agree with you on that, Miss Ethel. My poor rump hasn't been so sore since I was a girl caught licking honey out of my mother's mason jars."

Ethel laughed, a response that seemed to please the homely servant woman.

"You know, I've heard that since the island unioned with Canada, the prospect of a railroad may be high," Beulah added.

"Right you are, Miss Murphy. A railroad would sure make traveling by land much easier, especially for farmers inland who need to transport goods." Al paused and spat again, mumbling to the horses as the road dipped between a trench. Weeds and briars knotted in a tangle over the high arched banks around them as water splashed along the mud-caked spokes of the wagon wheels. Dandelions, ever-present and hearty, grew along the grassy edge where spongy topsoil turned from moistened cake and roots to matted alders.

"I think I'd like to take a train someday."

"Over the Princess of Wales, Miss Arsenault?"

Beulah huffed and would have spoken if not for Ethel's interruption. "Yes, Mr. Carlow," she said, patting at Miss Murphy's hand that was still hovering above her own. "I'm afraid I get uneasy when aboard a ship. I find it rather unsettling."

"Unsettling, Miss. Arsenault?"

Ethel nodded, watching as they climbed the banks. The Yorke River, bisected with a wooden bridge, shone in the distance like cathedral glass. "Yes. My late fiancé, Roland Diggory, was lost at sea some time ago. Perhaps you may find it absurd, Mr. Carlow, but I've since decided I would rather not be aboard a ship. Ever. Even if it means I shall never leave the island."

Fritz harrumphed, "Not absurd," and blew out a cloud of smoke that meandered into the carriage. Ethel found it welcoming.

"A-apologies, Miss. I wasn't aware of the circumstances."

"And why would you be, Mr. Carlow?" Beulah interrupted, sitting forward in her seat, if not to rearrange her bottom, then to emphasize her point. "You're here to drive the wagon! Not to bother us with noisome questions and prattle! If I were your employer, I would definitely be keeping a close eye on you. I suspect you fill your days with loafing and gamboling and chewing that ungodly tobacco. You've every known indication of a rascal, Mr. Carlow, and you shan't get the better of me."

Al Carlow laughed, and Ethel couldn't help but join him.

Beulah grinned and sat back, pursing her pouty lips. "At least when the railroad's built, we won't have to worry about tolerating the presence of riffraff, eh Miss Ethel?" she said with a wink.

The carriage bounced, and both ladies lurched in their seats as the wheels fell into deep ruts before skidding onward.

"You did that on purpose, Mr. Carlow," Beulah roared, pulling at a strand of auburn hair that had fallen out from under the short rim of her straw hat.

"Terrible sorry, Miss Arsenault. These roads are treacherous. Tell your servant girl to pipe down, won't you? She's awful distracting."

It's hard to be melancholy with such vibrant travel companions. Ethel couldn't help but feel lifted despite the dreary weather. Even Miss Murphy's constant bickering with Aloysius reminded her of the squabbling blue jays near her home in Green's Shore. Ethel wondered if perhaps she would return there before summer ended.

Looking down at the floor of the carriage, Ethel opened a small Gladstone bag. Inside the stiff, chapped cowhide case were a few books, a pocketbook, and a leather-bound journal stuffed with a bundle of stamped envelopes. Her brother had sent a missive several weeks ago, begging for her to visit, confessing that he was worried about Dolly during all his time away on business. The letter was there amidst a few others.

She picked out a book and turned the pages of Louisa May Alcott's well-read *Little Women* until it settled on chapter four. Ethel had only met Dolly on a handful of occasions, but it had never been anything more than the proper pleasantries exchanged between distant relatives. The young lady seemed a bundle of energy, bright and lovely, and as optimistic as a rainbow on a wet day.

Though Ethel and Dolly were of a similar age, they couldn't have been any more dissimilar. That her brother Ernest had thought Ethel could even come close to keeping his new bride company was a laugh. Ethel was, by her own definition, a guttering candlestick next to the glowing hearth that was Dolly Arsenault, but now that Ethel was alone and their parents were gone, she had no reason to refuse her brother or his invitation to Charlottetown. She had hoped that refusing to board a ship may have thwarted Ernest's will to have her there at the earliest convenience.

When the horses finally stalled at the mouth of Moor's Bridge, Ethel looked up from her book to catch a glimpse of the few small boats and punts that made a wharf out of the right flank of the crossing. Men were loading goods and produce to be transported from Cornwall to Charlottetown, while a few other carriages meandered across the narrow wooden expanse.

The bridge was like an old man's belt. It spanned the full belly of the Yorke River, hardly able to withstand the small amount of traffic that crossed it. The bridge had been destroyed by ice a few years ago, but despite being rebuilt, it still appeared too narrow for more than one large carriage at a time.

"I heard a parish priest that lives in Rustico brought this horseless wagon to the island a little while ago. Imagine that, Miss

Ethel! Being pulled around by something that runs on fuel and bric-a-brac."

"They can leave those damned terror wagons where they got 'em if you ask me," Mr. Carlow interrupted, spurring the horses onward as the bridge cleared of passing stagecoaches. "All they'll do is scare the horses, the children, and rough up the roads. Can you imagine?" He spat again. "I certainly hope I'll never have to."

Beulah tutted but didn't argue as she sat back and stared out the window.

Having read the same paragraph several times with no understanding of the words upon the page, Ethel thought to put her book down and engage in conversation. When she looked up, Beulah had already slumped into a midmorning nap, lulled to sleep by the horses.

Ethel watched as the waves hummed along the glassy back of the river, kicked up by water bugs and the occasional swaying of the bobbing boats. Roland would have loved a seabound journey to Charlottetown. She could picture him at the prow, his topcoat struggling to engulf the playful breeze that flung water and foam to bead upon his spectacles.

I've been widowed before marriage...

And yet, despite the clockwork clatter of the horses upon the wooden bridge, time had stopped since Roland's death. Perhaps Dolly's sunny disposition would help shed the dreary forecast Ethel Arsenault had resigned to herself.

Roland would have loved the journey to Charlottetown. So, perhaps then, I ought to enjoy it too.

Ethel skipped to chapter five in her book, resolved to finish it before they reached their destination. Overhead the sky grew darker. Across from her, Beulah slept, as restless as the dead.

Chapter 2

By midday, the coach had carried them beyond the rural gridwork of outlying farmlands that spilled from the core of Charlottetown. Though the quilt of green, yellow, and red fields had succumbed to urban development, the city was organised in rows upon rows of civic blocks pinned between muck-filled roads and hitching rails. The usual clip-clopping of the horses was instead a slapping of mud mingled with the slush of passing carriages. Smart-dressed pedestrians meandered along the brick buildings that stood like a fortress of commerce on either side of the city's streets. They stuck to the wooden sidewalks and planks that laid atop the gummy streetways, careful to mind the passing stagecoach.

The smell of the countryside was carried in by the trot of horses, though as Ethel leant out her window to gawk at the jigsaw of urban wonders, she inhaled the fresh scent of perfume from within the miasma of wet dirt. It waved hello from off the decorated hats of the women and girls who wandered the world in their colourful promenade costumes, even despite the swampy muck. Ethel couldn't help but sigh at the sight of them as she pulled at her black scalloped cape. Ethel had gotten so thin as of late, that she hoped her brother would recognize her.

"They've a store for everything here, eh Miss Ethel?" Beulah was round-eyed as she leant out the opposite side of the carriage to read the myriad of signs posted between the rows of arched windows. Cobblers, bakers, clothiers, and medical halls. Hardware, stovers, tinware, and some shops named for the people who owned them.

"I suppose they must label everything so that no one gets lost," Ethel mused, watching as a gaggle of men wandered towards a pub in a swagger.

They must be sailors... She sat back to smooth her skirts and fiddle with the pins that held her hair in place.

"You've been to Charlottetown before, haven't you, Miss Ethel?"

"Yes," Ethel said, "with my father, and later on with Ernest. Though it's been a while, and I've not seen the house the two conspired to build."

"Eden Hall's coming up, Miss!" Al hollered back, steering the horses west on Grafton Street. The smell of the water filled the air and settled on the tongue like a bladder of rockweed.

When her brother was married, their father had been ill, and the ceremony was conducted on the shores of Summerside for his sake. Eden Hall had been but a dream then, schemed up by her late father and brother as a wedding gift. She remembered seeing the drawings in the den—blueprints accompanied by scrawls and notes. Three stories, a verandah, and turret... Her father said it had to be in the style of a Queen Anne. Ernest agreed. What that entailed, Ethel could only guess at the time, but as the carriage pulled up and rounded the bend towards West Street, her family's conjurings were given life against the backdrop of the roiling Charlottetown Harbour.

Eden Hall was much more than three stories, a verandah, and a turret. While each complimented the general ambiance ushered from the manor's appearance, the plum cross-gabled roof, green trim, and ash grey asymmetrical facade reminded her of the orchards up past Richmond. It was a hearty building with conical bay windows on its right flank and a corner tower on the left. Above the expansive veranda trimmed in fluted stone columns, a balcony rose of much the same design.

Ethel could imagine Dolly waving out towards the road when company called, her sunny hair pinned yet gleaming from the sun that just barely managed to shine past the shaded rooftop. The thought brought a smile to Ethel's lips. She hoped with every business trip, Ernest found happiness in such a goodbye and homecoming.

A black, wrought iron fence outlined the perimeter of Eden Hall, though there were few neighbours along the corner of Grafton and West. The stables sat behind the manor.

Al Carlow and Fritz Humphrey stalled the carriage just outside the cobbled main path that led up to the front porch. Ethel heard both men grunt as they stood to stretch their backs, and Beulah echoed their relief when the front door to Eden Hall opened to welcome them.

"That can't be my sister, Ethel, without ink stains on her fingers or her nose buried in a book?" Ernest crashed out the front door like a cannon fire, hardly allowing enough time for Al to open the carriage door.

He proffered a helping hand and Ethel's smile grew in the presence of her brother. "Your affection is catching," she said as she stepped down into his warm embrace. "It's been too long, Ernest. The few short seasons we've had since your wedding seem like ages."

"And yet you seem smaller, Etty!" He stood back an arm's length to regard her, the severity of his dark brows and trimmed moustache eclipsed by soft, brown eyes and a round face.

"*You've* also gotten larger, Ernie," Ethel replied, sparing a glance towards his belly, disguised behind a tweed vest and open sack coat. She kept her chin down, biting back a cruel giggle as her eyes watched him from under the blackened rim of her mourning hat.

Ernest guffawed. "A time at Eden Hall will see you thicker as well, I suspect!" he said, clapping his hand around her shoulder as he tucked her underneath his arm. "And I haven't forgotten about you, Mr. Humphrey! I suspect Fritz, Al, and I will enjoy a shot of gin or two later this evening?"

As usual, the older man grunted, though there was an air of approval in Fritz Humphrey's eyes. Acting as translator, Al smiled and said, "Who could say no to an offer like that, Sir? I'll make sure the horses are well put to bed before any libations are thrown around."

"Good lad! And show Fritz a room he'll find comfortable." Ernest and Ethel were making their way up towards the large, snaking verandah when her brother peered over his shoulder to call back, "And I haven't forgotten about you either, Miss Murphy. I want to know all the trouble you and Ethel have gotten up to in my absence."

"No trouble at all Mr. Arsenault. But I'm afraid my poor backside begs for better pillows on the ride back." Beulah carried Ethel's Gladstone bag in her right hand whilst the other patted her rump in emphasis. Ethel was surprised to have forgotten her bag in the stagecoach.

"Hopefully, that will be a while yet." He leant down to mutter more privately. "Dolly has been quite eager for you to arrive, Etty. I'm afraid my business ventures often take me away from Eden Hall, and the poor dear is often left alone at the house.”

“The hall is magnificent. You and father really outdid yourselves.”

Ernest rumbled with another jolly laugh. “Yes, but I’m afraid its size takes a lot of getting used to. More women to fill the corridors will help Dolly settle in. She’s not quite used to something so grand.”

Neither was she, Ethel thought. Even her family home back in Summerside was not so elegant, but Ernest’s business in Charlottetown had been lucrative.

They stepped up onto the patio. The door to Eden Hall was solid mahogany, framed in stained glass with sidelight windows.

“When do you leave for Boston, brother?” Ethel asked, glancing back to Beulah to ensure the woman was following after them.

“I’m all set to leave in a few days. I wanted to make sure you were comfortable before I departed. Though servants often fill much of the space during the day, there are none that stay overnight, having homes in the city. Even now, only Adella comes regularly.” The initial reason Ernest had wanted her to come and stay at Eden Hall was because Dolly wasn’t used to the grandeur of a large house or estate. Ethel couldn’t imagine being in a great big place like Eden Hall all by herself. Though now that her parents were gone, it was only her and Beulah who stayed together at Greens Shore.

As they entered, the light from outside spilled inward to the foyer. Patterned green wallpaper, spotted with pink roses, kept the interior in perpetual spring, while dark stairs, coated in plush carpet, wound upwards to frame a hanging chandelier. Portraits of gardens and shipyards hung on the wall, while corridors spilled into surrounding rooms, lit by the natural sunlight that meandered in through the tall windows.

It was familiar, like the ghost of her father lived on in the wooden panels that bisected the emerald wallpaper. It was like stepping into a dream or through a portrait that you saw every day but never quite got a good look at it.

"This is lovely Ernes–"

"Is that Ethel? Ernie, you were supposed to let me know when she arrived." Dolly was a spark of vigour as she descended the stairs, in the process of pinning a diamond teardrop in one ear. Her hair was pinned loosely atop her head. Her ruffled blouse, buttoned in a high collar with a silver and garnet brooch, was tucked into a brown plaid skirt with twin pleats and secured with two rows of brass buttons. She portrayed a picture of youthful fashion, her soft features and charm emphasised by the light in Dolly's blue eyes.

"How was your trip here, Ethel?" Dolly asked, rushing into a warm and familiar embrace that seemed natural for her. Ernest stumbled aside in an attempt to accommodate his young wife, while Ethel tensed, caught off guard by the merry hello.

"It went well, thank you."

"I know you have an aversion to the water, Etty, but next time you must simply take the boat. The ride here has left you looking awfully tired." Dolly pressed the pads of her fingers beneath Ethel's chin in an effort to lift it higher for examination. Dolly's face turned into a portrait of concern, made genuine by the softness of her eyes and parted mouth. Ethel was touched by the woman's care. It seemed maternal in nature, despite Dolly being younger in age.

Ethel grasped her sister's-in-law's hand and held it between her own. Her eyes were rather heavy, but she became determined to mirror a bit of the sun and sparkle that was emitting from her sister-in-law.

"Thank you for your concern, but I'm fine. Truly. It's nothing a nap won't cure." Dolly glanced at Ethel's mourning attire and pursed her lips into a thin line. Before the silence could darken, Ernest shook his head.

"Hear that, Dolly? Our old Ethel is as tough as aged leather."

"I wouldn't have put it quite so poetically, perhaps," Ethel muttered, glancing behind her as Beulah chuckled.

Ernest smiled so big his top teeth were exposed. "Well, you were ever the poet in the family, Ethel," Ernest replied, gesturing towards the stairs. "Come, I'll show you and Beulah to your rooms on the second floor so you may rest and unpack."

Dolly jumped, moving from her place before the stairs to her husband's side. Her eyes widened like sea pearls, and her cheeks went flush despite the cool air that had shifted inside when the door had opened.

"Oh, Ernie, do you think it would be unfathomable to dine at the Windmill tonight? I've heard a lot of the ships have come in, and it would be simply beautiful to dine on the docks this evening." Dolly turned to include Ethel in the conversation. "Ethel, you would love it. The view from the second-floor window would certainly inspire any poet!"

Ernest looked askance at his sister with an unsure grin. "Well, Dolly... I have some business to attend to at the Windmill tonight—"

"I know." Dolly beamed. "And we wouldn't dare get underfoot. After we dine, I can show Ethel to the landing. It's right outside, after all."

"With all the sailors afoot?"

Dolly waved her hand. An emerald cluster sparkled upon a golden bangle dangling from her delicate wrist. "I'm sure we could arrange a chaperone if you're worried, dear. But there will be plenty of constables about to ensure no ruckus is made, what with all the ships coming in."

Ethel muffled a phantom laugh in her fist as Ernest looked to her to dissuade his assiduous, young wife. When it was obvious she would not come to his aid, Ernest opened his arms, waffling excuses. "I'm sure Ethel would like some time to rest and unpack, Dear, and we can't leave her alone when she's only just arrived..."

"I don't mind getting settled for you, Miss Ethel. There are a few hours before supper, so you'd have time enough to get ready and have a nap, if you wished."

Ethel couldn't help but laugh at the face her brother pulled at poor Beulah, but as always, the young lady was unfazed. "It would also give me a bit of time to get familiar with the house while you three are gone."

Dolly squeaked with cheer, moving past her husband to face Miss Murphy as though the verdict had been chosen. "Quite right, Miss Murphy. Oh, Ethel won't you please agree to come?"

Dolly was grasping her arm again, a flurry of eagerness between the four of them. Looking past the young girl's sunny locks and elegant attire, Ethel saw her brother's spent resolve sputter in a drawn-out sigh and sheepish shrug behind her.

"It sounds wonderful, Dolly. I would be most pleased to accompany you."

The echo of Dolly's mirth seemed to brighten the dull light petering in through the windowpanes. And as they bounded up the stairs, arm in arm, leaving Ernest to contemplate his new evening plans, Ethel couldn't help but feel warmed in the wake of her sister-in-law.

"The room down the hall is yours, Beulah. I know how much of a friend you are to Ethel, so I thought you'd both enjoy being in close proximity. There is one other girl who was staying overnight downstairs in the servant's quarters, but she's already headed home to visit her mother."

The wallpaper continued up from the first floor, though here it was speckled with large, hand-drawn portraits and mirrors, along with one grandfather clock standing sentinel between two bedroom doors.

"Do most of the maids come in during the morning, Mrs. Arsenault?"

"Precisely. Around five o'clock. And Aloysius stays in a room off the stables most nights. You can find him there if something goes amiss in the night and Ernest isn't around."

Beulah nodded, glancing towards Ethel as the bedroom off the right side of the hall was opened. Ethel would be staying on the second floor of the Queen Anne's turret. A large, four-poster bed with heavy curtains sat against the far wall, soaking up the sunlight that poured in streams along the floor. Beige walls sectioned by wooden panels were adorned with portraits of birds standing idle in egg-shaped frames. The fireplace was next to the bed, the flame low, while a mirror, vanity, and dresser stood beyond the borders of a plush green carpet. There was a lounger at the end of the bed, as well as a few books that looked to have been brought up from downstairs. Outside the four, front-facing windows, the sea was a blue grey, like cobalt on a dour morning.

"I'll have Aloysius and Fritz bring up the rest of your stuff, and Beulah can unpack when we leave. I'm sure you'll want to refresh and change after your nap."

"I best go make sure that the rascal doesn't break something," Beulah barked, setting Ethel's Gladstone bag on the bed before leaving through the doorway. Ethel watched her go and tried to avoid the look in Dolly's eyes as the young woman regarded her black dress from toe to chest.

"Ethel," she began as soon as they were alone, "how long has—I mean, it's been well over a year, has it not?"

Ethel looked away, expecting the question and yet, not quite prepared to answer it. She had been in mourning longer than Ernest and Dolly had been wed. But despite the time, and the fact that Roland had never been her husband, Ethel wasn't ready to let him go.

She didn't wish to snuff out Dolly's bright enthusiasm, however, so grasping her by the hand, Ethel nodded. "My old clothes don't fit, is all, and I've been too busy to have them tailored."

Dolly's smile returned, and Ethel was glad to have been the one to inspire it. "We shall have to go shopping. I've a few dresses that you could have in the meantime, if Beulah is good at sewing."

"Very good," Ethel agreed, her heart sinking. Dolly's enthusiasm soared, but despite unceremoniously getting caught up in it, Ethel found herself short of breath.

"I'll take a look while you rest. If you need anything, be sure to let me know. Our room is upstairs on the third floor, and the parlour is downstairs next to the study. That's where Ernest keeps himself most days when he's not at work."

She left in a whirl of excitement, leaving Ethel to her own gloomy thoughts while reeling from the sunny storm that was Dolly's cloying demeanour. Though she could hear the tumult from downstairs, Ethel closed the door to her room, expecting that Beulah would handle the luggage and see that she was not disturbed.

Ethel lay upon the bed and stared up into the canopy. As the noise dimmed and the soft patter of rain ticked like moments against the windowpanes, she closed her eyes. Thinking of Roland as the world spun in circles, she slept amid the heart of it all at Eden Hall.

Chapter 3

Though Ethel had only a glance into her brother's life in Charlottetown, even that cursory peek was enough to overwhelm the senses. The few precious hours before they were to head out to the docks for supper was the only respite Ethel had to rest and recharge her social metre. She slept a little, read some more, then washed her face and repinned her hair before starting chapter six of her book. She hadn't gotten very far when she heard a knock at her chamber door. Ethel marked the page, then rose, inhaling deep and readying a smile for her beloved sister-in-law.

Dolly looked resplendent in her evening gown, and though she wore the same attire she had greeted Ethel in earlier this afternoon, her face was dusted with rice powder and stained at the apples of her cheeks with a natural-looking rouge. Dolly held a gown in one arm, and Ethel's maid, Beulah, stood behind her, an apologetic expression awkwardly plastered upon the young lady's face.

"I've found a gown for you to wear, Ethel," Dolly exclaimed, rushing inside the room like a tsunami. Miss Murphy was on her heels like an ensnared piece of debris. "I had it made for my sister's birthday half a year ago, but she fell pregnant and I thought it in poor taste to gift it to her." She laid it on the bed, and it looked like a scar against the pale cream of the linens.

The pink gown had a lace chiffon bodice trimmed in pearl detail and a ruffled neckline. Puffed sleeves ending in a tightened cuff were embroidered in baby's breath, while flowers of the same sort were situated in a broad cartwheel chapeau of a similar hue.

It was beautiful, made for a girl of vibrant youth, flowering in the prime of her life. But despite her age and unwed status, Ethel would have rather been a darkened nook in Eden Hall than a garden bouquet.

"This is... lovely." Ethel ran her fingers over the fitted skirt, at odds at what words she could say to keep her from wearing it. "But if this was a gift for your sister, I couldn't possibly—"

"Of course you can. Mary-Beth is much too thick to wear it now, and probably always will be. See it as a gift. We are sisters too, after all." Dolly turned away, looking in the vanity drawer for a handkerchief.

"Beulah says you don't often wear any stain on your cheeks or lips, but I've some beet juice to liven up your complexion. It's simply magic, and with but a few dabs here and there, no one can even tell it's not completely natural."

Dolly took a small, stoppered vial Beulah had been holding and directed the robust woman towards the gown upon the bed. Ethel's teeth were hurting beneath her smile, but she nodded as Miss Murphy moved to redress her. Ethel couldn't remember ever wearing a gown so fine and wondered why, with so much natural beauty, Dolly would wear anything at all upon her face. Ethel did not want to seem rude or ungrateful, so she played doll while her in-law fussed, tutted, and beamed at Ethel's transformation.

"Are you ladies ready yet?" Ernest called from the foyer.

Dolly stepped back, clapping her hands in earnest. "Lovely," she said with glassy eyes. Outside, the rain had stopped, and the warm smear of the falling sun brushed the sky like wet paint. Ethel felt the warmth at her back, though it did little to thaw her stiffened limbs, even when Dolly rushed to embrace her.

"I'm so glad you've come, Ethel. Today has already been the greatest of days."

"Dolly!"

The young woman stepped back, glancing one more time at Ethel's attire before turning on her heel to leave. "We're coming, Dear," she called.

"I don't wish to be late for dinner," Ernest explained with merry cheer.

"*Unfashionably* late, you mean." Already Dolly was a phantom down the hall, and standing next to her maid, Ethel inhaled as though for the first time, wondering how long she was to be haunted by the pretty lady of Eden Hall.

"Are you all right, Miss Ethel?" Beulah asked, making a face that implied her wariness over the young Mrs. Arsenault.

"Fine," Ethel replied, her mouth relaxing into a natural grin. "Admittedly, a bit uncomfortable, but fine just the same."

"You look like a posy." There was no venom in her words, though Ethel couldn't help but laugh.

"A glass one, perhaps. Will you be all right while we're gone?"

Beulah nodded, rolling up one sleeve as her mirth made plump mounds of her cheeks. "Absolutely. After the last few hours, a bit of quiet will do me good. I'll make the room up while you're gone, Miss Ethel. You enjoy yourself. Certainly, you deserve it."

* * *

Though the Windmill was but a few blocks from Eden Hall, Ernest had summoned a cab to take them down towards the dockyard. The mud was thick still, and already the planks that served as a pedestrian walkway were soiled beyond what was manageable. The harbour was like a spill of black paint. The stars were captured in the waves and the foamy swells, where the

Hillsborough River collided into the Charlottetown Harbour. Wharfs stuck out from Water Street like the teeth of a lady's comb, raking in rockweed and barnacles that clung to the ship-laden moors and delivered the briny scent of the sea inland.

Though the air had been cold when Ethel arrived, it was balmy now. The warmth hugged her skin like a wax film but locked the chill in her bones. Inside the restaurant, they sat before a set of French doors that opened to a balcony spanning the entire length of the building's facade. The water loomed like empty space from beyond the second-floor windows, while the reflection in the glass let Ethel see the other diners in the farther corners of the room.

When they arrived, the table was set and adorned in white linen. An array of silk blossoms interspersed with fragrant wildflowers quivered beneath the candlelight that hung from globes upon the ceiling. Behind them, close to the stairs that led down to the first story, was a bar. Despite the hour, it was sparsely occupied. Though Ernest had explained on the ride over that they were to be accompanied by a few other gentlemen, the three of them had been the first to arrive.

"This place is lovely," Ethel said, glancing around the dining room. Her brother smiled from across the rectangular table, while Dolly turned to glance out the French doors towards the harbour.

"I think I'll have a chat with the sommelier over the choice of wine," she said, having hardly sat before she stood to excuse herself. Ernest laughed, nodding as his young wife gathered her skirts to head for the bar. "Can I get you a drink, dear?" she asked.

"A glass of gin."

"With lime?"

He made a face, causing Ethel to chuckle. Though Ernest may have been older now, more distinguished from his youth, she was happy to see that the brother she loved was still there. Though perhaps a bit chubbier than before.

"Anything for you, Ethel?" Dolly asked, placing her hand on Ethel's shoulder.

Ethel shook her head, watching from the reflection in the glass as Dolly moved back towards the bar. The man there seemed to know her, his smile a large slash across his face as he moved closer in order to converse at length.

"Did Dolly gift you that gown?" Ernest asked, shocking Ethel from her reverie as she looked across the table towards him. Ernest was fetching a small cigar from a silver case, his merry blue eyes trained on hers as she glanced down at her attire.

"Yes. I'm afraid it may be a bit too lavish for me. Certainly, the lace would get caught on every snag and stray nail if I were to wear it at home."

Ernest laughed as he picked up a candlestick to light the end of his evening smoke. Waving the fog from his exhale, he glanced at the bundle of wildflowers on the table and nodded. "*Much* too lavish, but lovely all the same," he said, letting the silence linger like the smoke between them, before adding, "and much better than black." Ethel's smile faded, though she was careful not to let it vanish as Ernest continued on, "I must admit, I was worried when I first saw you, Ethel. *Have* you been all right? Perhaps I shouldn't have left Summerside so soon after the funeral?"

She saw the worry in his eyes, souring the youthful mirth that reminded her of the sunny days playing in the potato fields and catching dragonflies. He may have been a man now, with business aplenty, a wife and estate, but the boy within him shone through like wet ink on an aged journal.

"Sometimes I feel a bit lonely," Ethel admitted, thinking honesty would help to conceal the true melancholy she harboured. "After Mother and Father, and of course Roland, I..." she traced the embroidery on the tablecloth, hoping the pattern would lead her to an answer that would assuage Ernest's concerns, "It's given me a lot of time to read and write. I'm not sure what I would have done without Beulah to run the household, but I am very appreciative of her. I think time away from Summerside will do me good. Dolly seems the type to keep one busy, and after spending months lost to thought and literature, it will be nice to go shopping for a few more gowns."

Ernest smiled, concern hanging from the corners of his eyes, but only just. "A threefold benefit, your arrival," he said, taking another inhale. "While you two entertain each other, I can shuffle off to make the money you'll likely spend in my absence." He chuckled, nodding to the waiter who brought over a glass of gin. From the reflection, Ethel could see Dolly still busy at the bar, conversing with the sommelier.

"How *have* you been doing, Ernest? How is life in Charlottetown? With Dolly?"

He took a drink, pausing as though to consider the taste. "Busy. Business is booming, though with talk of a railroad and of us joining the Canadian Confederation, I suspect there will be a lot of change on the horizon. Luckily for me, Prince Edward Island shall always be in need of boats." He looked past her now, regarding Dolly over by the bar. "Though Dolly and I met in Charlottetown, I'm afraid she's not used to living so often by herself. Business takes me away a lot," he explained, "and having grown up with three sisters, I'm afraid Eden Hall is a bit too big for her. Once a few children come along—"

"You have to be home more often if you want to think about children, Ernest." Ethel laughed, watching as her brother coughed through another mouthful of gin.

"I suppose you're right about that," he replied after a moment, wiping his mouth as a flush gathered in the apples of his cheeks. "Of course, when they do come along, they'll need to know their Auntie Etty."

The thought made her pause and looking down at one of the silver spoons left out on the table, Ethel felt her sadness still in the wake of Ernest's words. *A niece or nephew. A child. Someone to read to and love. Auntie Etty...* "I'd like to know them too," she said. "You ought to have a lot, of course... to fill that home of yours."

"One for each day of the week?"

Ethel nodded. "As long as I still have a room for visiting, lest you have to build on— and they can come to Green's Shore at the start of fall for the potato harvest."

"Hard work is essential for good living," Ernest agreed.

The thought thrilled her, so much so that she didn't notice Dolly returning from the bar with another young man.

"The barkeep was just promising something rather robust for the table when, as though on que, Constable Bertram arrived."

The young man smiled as Ernest leapt up to greet him. The expression looked forced and awkward on a face so angled and serious.

"I'm sorry to keep you waiting," he began, glancing towards Ethel as Dolly left to take her seat. He looked no older than thirty, with an impeccably groomed moustache that carried the bulk of his age. As he sat beside her and introductions were made, Ethel couldn't help but note the smell of dust wafting from his very expensive, tailored suit.

"My sister Ethel is visiting for a while. Etty, this is Constable Andrew Bertram, he helps with the many legalities involving the shipping trade."

"Keeping the sailors in line, mostly." Bertram nodded, offering her another lopsided smile that matched his bowtie.

"Modesty doesn't suit you, Sir," Dolly replied.

Three other gentlemen joined them after a while. They were older than the first, with expensive cologne that disguised the scent of the constable's dusty suit. All three were business associates of her brother's, and quite polite despite their friendly rowdiness towards each other. As the lot of them conversed, discussing matters over full plates and half-empty wineglasses, Ethel found herself oddly pleased to be sitting beside Andrew Bertram. Though he weighed in on the conversations when prompted, the constable was otherwise quiet, and she felt less the imposter because of his presence.

A dusty suit and borrowed dress… sat in a nobleman's wardrobe.

"Can I get you anything else, Gentlemen?" the waiter asked as Ernest passed around cigars.

"Whiskey! Shall we enjoy it on the verandah, Gentlemen?" Ernest glanced around the table.

The other men agreed, though Ethel noticed the constable's response came only after he was personally invited.

"Well then, if you don't mind, I think I'll take Ethel to see the harbour." Dolly held her wine glass as she stood, though it had been only sipped at once or twice during dinner.

"By yourselves?" Bertram asked with a glance to Ernest who regarded his wife then sister over the rim of his finished gin.

Dolly fanned her fingers before the spark of concern could catch. "We are simply crossing the road, Constable. The only threat to us shall be the mud, I suspect. My husband will be able to see us from the verandah, so long as he paces himself. Besides, business talk is rather tiring for the fairer sex."

"Let them go, Bertram!" one of the other gents replied, looking clownish as the large cigar bobbed as if in lecture from between his lips.

Tipped over the fence by his companion's retort, Ernest nodded and stood from his seat. "It'll be all right. Ethel is quite capable of taking care of herself, and if anything *were* to happen, well... Dolly would surely deafen us all with her screams." The three gents laughed as Ernest soaked a playful strike from his posturing wife. "The lamp lighters have already been around, so we can keep an eye on them."

Constable Bertram looked unsure, but with Ernest's consent, Dolly stood to don a shawl. "Come now, Ethel. The harbour is beautiful this time of night. We should be able to see the light from the lighthouse and the ships unloading from the wharfs."

Ethel followed along, watching as the five men left to resume their conversation on the balcony. Outside, the sea whispered against the docks like a mother shushing her child to sleep. Lanterns glittered along the roadside, some winking in constellations over the black expanse of water where boats floated like crowns upon the sea.

Across from the Windmill, the cobbled street yawned into an open plaza. Framed in sparkling light posts and stone flowerpots, Ethel was certain the area would be a hub of merchant stalls and produce during the day. There were a few benches overlooking the water that sat behind a timber fence, several small buildings, and pubs seeking to exploit the lovely view during the day.

Dolly strode ahead, the wind filling her skirts and drawing them back in phantom whirls as she leant over the rail to regard the water. "I love when the boats come in," she said, tipping her chin to inhale the air. "Charlottetown feels so lively when its wharves are full."

Ethel settled herself upon a bench and tucked the hem of her dress between her calves to keep the wind away. She didn't envy the men upon those boats, even though the view from the docks was spectacular. Ethel imagined being on the deck of a ship in the dead of night must be akin to being lost in space. Even with the floating boards beneath her feet, she'd feel lost, disoriented, and overwhelmed.

She placed a hand on her stomach and wondered if perhaps her meal wasn't settling right.

"Aren't you going to come watch, Ethel?" Dolly asked, her face glowing.

"I'm all right here." She smiled, glad to be silhouetted by the lights behind her.

Dolly inhaled and shook her head before returning her eyes to the water. "I'm so glad you've come, Ethel, even if it might not be the best time."

"What do you mean?"

She leant over the rail, watching as the light from the Point Prim lighthouse shone like the north star from across the bay. "Mother and Father moved across the island to Bloomfield. My sisters are all gone... wed and carried away to a happily ever after—much deserved, I should add—but despite my own obvious prosperity: Ernest, Eden Hall, living in this wonderful city... I can't help but feel a bit off—lonely."

Dolly turned around but stared down at the cobbles. The night had brought in the fog, and so the stones were damp and shining like a dove's eye. "You read. Ernest has told me that you've read a great many books."

Ethel paused, then said, "I suppose I've read a few." She felt cumbersome beneath the young lady's glare.

Dolly nodded. "I've not read many, but the ones I have seem to all inevitably end. I am left wondering what the characters do after they are married and happy and have it all." She turned again to look out at the water, her question abandoned.

Ethel followed Dolly's gaze but found her heart aching. She wanted to comfort her, do something about the dour pall that had fallen over such a vibrant, young lady. But all Ethel could think of was Roland, *her* loss, her *ending*, and how no one could understand because it was a whole lot more than a few words on a page.

"I think—" Ethel began, tightening her arms around her torso to keep herself together, "that when they say happily ever after, what the author truly means is nothing of dire consequence. Of course, there will always be sad times, but through it all, the main protagonists are unified. Together. But you're talking romance novels only, Dolly. Some stories *start* at a happy ending. Some couples go on to have fantastic adventures, and some stories still—"

End in tragedies, she thought.

"I'm sorry."

Ethel inhaled, startled as Dolly sat on a bench and wrapped her shawl around her shoulders. "You've no reason to comfort me. My problems are small and smaller still, now that you've arrived." She smiled and looked over the harbour. "We are sisters, you and I. At least, I hope you will see me as such."

Ethel nodded and took the girl's hands. They were cold, and Dolly's face was only half illuminated now that she sat upon the bench. "I've nothing to lose by gaining a sister. You can confide in me, Dolly. I won't judge you for it."

"And I you, Ethel." Dolly tipped her head down, as though to try and see past the night that obscured her companion's features.

Ethel looked away. There was hope in her chest now. It took away a bit of the pain she was feeling. "Thank you, Dolly, but it's getting late. We've many days ahead to talk?"

The levity in her voice had caught Dolly's heels, and the woman swooped up like brier in the wind. "Yes, of course! Many, *many* days. We'll go back in just a moment. I just want to see if the Princess of Wales has docked yet."

Ethel had to laugh, and though still wary of the water and its cluster of winking stars, she stood from the bench to look. "How could you even tell with everything so dark?"

"Faith," Dolly replied, as a few loose curls streamed from the nape of her neck like a kite ribbon. "It's strongest in the blind, after all."

Ethel sighed and gathered both shawls around her shoulders.

Chapter 4

The night got colder as they headed back towards the Windmill, and though Ernest was inebriated, he hailed a coach to take them to Eden Hall. Constable Bertram stayed behind as they clambered into the stagecoach, helping both herself and Dolly to settle in graciously with gowns intact. He looked as sober as he had been in the company of the other three gentlemen earlier in the evening, though Ethel was sure she smelled a bit of wine on his breath when he said goodbye. It complimented his dusty attire.

When they returned, Ernest bid them goodnight, excusing himself to go and speak with Mr. Humphrey and Aloysius in the stables. It was just past nine in the evening when Dolly and Ethel parted ways in the hall, and Ethel was glad to see her room made up. Beulah had unpacked all her necessities and clothing, stored them away and turned down her bed. A humble fire burned in the fireplace, and a window had been cracked to let in a bit of air and expel some of the heat.

I'm not sure I've ever felt so tired.

Ethel changed into her bedclothes. It had been such a long day, and she wondered if all her time at Eden Hall would be so exhausting. "Perhaps I'm being overly dramatic," she said aloud as she hung up the gown Dolly had so generously gifted. Ethel had been wallowing in dim misery for so long that she supposed the sunny glee Dolly offered would take some getting used to. She *had* taken to the girl. Who could not?

Despite her fatigue, Ethel smiled, resolved to find her cheer before the morning sun climbed the sky. Her Gladstone bag sat at the foot of the bed, and as she slipped beneath the covers, she retrieved her book.

A few more chapters before bed, I think. She read aloud till chapter nine and fell asleep at fourteen. There was the sound of bells tolling in the distance, dismissed by the roar of the tide and clap of wet logs burning to char in the hearth.

She woke in darkness to the whisper of phantoms.

* * *

The seas were churlish and pulled the rockweed from their roots to hover in a canopy atop the water's surface. The bloated bladders that hung like beads from the rocking current, snapped and burst. The foam and bubbles entombed within their bellies, scorched her hands as Ethel struggled to swim, but her feet were anchored in place, buried beneath the rubble and dirt of the harbour.

She was almost there. Her fingertips skimmed the roiling plane of water that defined the sky from its briny depths. But every time she thought she'd been let free, the rockweed moved to curtain her nails and wrap about her fingers, and the seabed inhaled to pull her deeper.

Her lungs were full, her belly bulging and pregnant with water. She was wearing Dolly's dress, and the pink chiffon crashed in the undertow like battered netting, catching at barnacles and broken shells.

Panic was a rabid beast inside her, but for all her thrashing and pulling and twisting, the pain of gulping in more water with every manic scream was a torrid realisation cut with dread.

Then the surface fell away. The little pockets of light that were almost imperceptible between the clotted bundles of seaweed, turned to darkness. As though filling its basin from some unknown source, the waterline rose until she could no longer see it. Her body bobbed in the current, but as the bonds at her ankles fell slack, she turned with stinging eyes to stare at Roland's face.

His cheeks were swollen, his pallor ashen and blue. Small fish picked at the grime within his short-trimmed hair and beard, while black roe spilled like spume from out of his mouth.

He was buried in the seabed. His tomb of clams and periwinkles lined the walls of an empty casket alongside him. Ethel screamed and heard herself cry as her addled body floated upwards to finally breach the water's surface, but as she clawed for purchase, pain shot through her belly.

* * *

The room was dark and her vision blurry as her eyes snapped open. Ethel sat up, like a twig broken in the path of phantom footsteps. Her chest sputtered from the adrenaline spawned from her nightmares, but as she grasped her breast and let her eyes adjust, Ethel's body settled amidst the hill-like coverlets of Eden Hall.

The curtains had been drawn. The copper bed-warmer between the sheets was a fading heat against the chill that sat outside the thick canopy of her four-post bed. As Ethel settled, satisfied to pull herself beneath the blankets and wish away her foul dreams, she hesitated, a pain in her belly and a noise in the hall directing her glance.

"Hello?" she whispered, sure she had heard a voice. A staccato beat, like the thrum of a racing heart, stampeded in her ears. It was outside in the hall, then in the walls, and as she listened, its rhythm transformed to a drawn out moan from the floorboards.

50

"Is someone there?" she called, waiting for the response of her bedroom door. Though Ethel could not see past the heavy hung drapes of her bed, she knew it was there, just beyond.

She waited, straining to hear the sound of the door opening. Thoughts of her nightmares wove fright in her mind, and she wondered at the ghosts that would haunt Eden Hall.

What spirit would dwell in a manor so young, lest it came in the heart of a guest?

Silence lingered like a loathsome smell. Moving to investigate, Ethel stalled at the sense of something amiss. She reached below to pat at herself and groaned at the moisture within.

Her woman's cycle had started, and it bloomed over the sheets in deep red, clotted carnations.

She sighed. "Oh, Lord hairy... what a nuisance," Ethel muttered, looking beyond the curtains with a dismissive frown. She thought about rousing Beulah but decided against it. The woman would be tired after a long day of unpacking, and there was no need to disturb her when Ethel could manage.

She stood and shivered from the cold lying in wait outside the walls of her bedroom curtains. Forgetting her fears and suspicions, Ethel fetched her apron from her wardrobe, and secured it in place before removing her gown to be laundered. She donned a new nightdress and stripped what sheets had been fouled, before finding another blanket from the bottom of her dresser to lay across the mattress.

Her hands were cold when she'd finished and barely warmed when she blew into them. But staring at the made-up bed and then the hearth where embers cooled, Ethel looked back to the door that lay undisturbed, frowned, and bit her lip.

She was sure of hearing voices, muffled and quiet, but rambunctious, like children at play when they were meant to be sleeping. She crept to the door on the balls of her feet, her long hair draping down her back like a veil. Though the hinges groaned from use, Ethel was able to slide through a lithe opening into the hall. The grandfather clock ticked past one in the morning, its regal face adorned in shadow. The paintings on the wall were but dismal squares. A chill like an icy hand gripped the back of Ethel's neck, causing the skin on her arms to prickle, but as the clattering sounds of movement echoed from down the stairs, her feet descended the staircase as her ears strained to listen.

Go back to bed.

Her heart leapt, as though it had been wrenched at from behind. Ethel turned, her eyes scanning the hall as her body leant back towards the railing. Nobody was there, and yet as her breath puffed like mad ghosts from between her lips, she was sure she had heard the voice. It was deep and final, a stout authority, not jovial like her brothers. It reminded her of Roland and pressing a fist to her chest as though warding off her nerves, she stared at a painting on the wall. A lone ship in a canvass of black waters. There was neither sun nor skies, just misty fog that clung as heavily as the darkness did to Eden Hall.

Ethel thought about returning to her room, wondering if her imaginations—spawned from dismal dreams–were giving way to ghoulish fancies. But the sounds from below chimed again, and steeling her grit, Ethel returned to the stairs, walking with fae-soft steps until she reached the bottom.

She passed the foyer, skirted the den, and glanced into Ernest's office where his books were askew. A candle sat upon his desk and another on his gun cabinet, but she didn't take them. They had long since guttered away. Ethel was amazed at how easily she guided herself through the house, recalling the blueprints and plans her father had managed to drape across every available space. To every last detail, the manor complied, though it wasn't until Ethel had wandered towards the back of the house that she had spied a light.

The kitchens were lit, and the warmth of the stove permeated the pantry and the small labyrinth of servant's corridors connecting outward.

Someone was speaking. A woman's voice.

"I can hear you, you know. You're barely discreet..." Ethel called out, rubbing her arms as they crossed over her front.

Dolly was at a table, a box opened in front of her. She was slicing limes, and a bottle of gin was set on the counter. She jumped at the sound, at Ethel's sudden appearance in the doorway. Her robe was opened and her hair was loosened into long, tight curls. Her nightgown dragged on the floor.

"Ethel! What are you doing up so late, my dear?" Dolly asked, laughing away her alarm as she smiled and dropped the knife to suckle at her fingers. She made a face from the sour juice of the citrus fruit. "I didn't wake you, did I?" Dolly asked, moving away from the counter.

There was a lantern on the table, the flame high, dressing the room in sunny light. Ethel exhaled. "I thought I heard a noise. Is everything all right? W-why are you up?"

Dolly nodded, backpedalling to retrieve her glass of gin and lime. "Quite all right," she began, "Ernest has a bit of indigestion. I thought this may help him to bed." She giggled, and Ethel watched the gin in the glass swirl with flecks of pulp.

"I thought I heard you speaking..."

Dolly paused, leaning in as though suspecting her to finish.

"You heard *me?*" She looked around, then spun to regard the space behind her. "There's no one here..." she said as she returned and paused to consider the notion. She glanced sideways before returning her stare, and whispered, "Are you sure you weren't dreaming?"

Was I? "I—" Ethel hesitated, watching as Dolly scanned the room with timid apprehension. Ethel could tell the concept of a voice was frightening her.

"I—uh... P-probably. You said that Ernest is sick?"

Dolly was relieved. She nodded her head.

"If he's sick, it probably has more to do with staying out late drinking with Fritz and Mr. Carlow."

"I would have to agree with that."

Dolly chuckled as she gathered the lantern and smiled as they both walked out from the kitchens.

"Well," she said, lacing her arm around Ethel's, "the hair of the dog that bit you, right?"

Ethel nodded but didn't relax. *What was the voice in the hallway?* Had her own demons and phantoms taken root in Eden Hall? A house her brother built, a legacy of her father, a home to dearest Dolly—spoiled by Ethel Arsenault—her black clothes and woeful mind and would-be-never husband, whose death had speared her heart.

Chapter 5

By morning, the sun had cut through the evening fog and coloured the sky a vibrant blueberry. Trees whispered the day's forecast, while birds filled their wings with the subtle breeze that blew in off the harbour. Ethel roused about nine, though despite her best efforts, was unable to sweep the dark circles from beneath her eyes. Dreams of Roland, of spectres in the night, lay packed in bags above her cheeks.

Beulah waved it off as a bad night in a foreign bed when she came in to take the laundry.

Ethel hoped Beulah was correct.

"My trip to Boston's been postponed," Ernest said at breakfast. He had fully dressed, but his collar was open and his coat slung over the chair. "Just for a few more days," he said, "but I thought since the day's nice, we'd all go out."

The dining room was bright. The bay windows that looked out onto the garden let the sun in to warm those who sat within its walls. The tea felt hearty in Ethel's stomach, combined with eggs and fried bacon.

Ernest was at the head of a small dining table, and a few delectable dishes had been laid out by the serving woman who had come in earlier in the day. Beulah was helping in the kitchens, while Dolly, still in her night robe, sat at Ernest's left. A cracked boiled egg, barely touched, was placed in front of her.

"I'm afraid I'm not feeling well today, Ernie," Dolly said, forcing a smile as she set the egg spoon down upon the table. "Perhaps you and Ethel could go on without me?"

Ernest looked sidelong, reaching across the table to place a concerned hand over his wife's. "It's not like you, Dolly. Are you all right? Should I call a doctor?"

Dolly shook her head. "I just didn't get enough sleep, I think."

Ethel frowned, wondering if the ghosts that had haunted her sleep had also haunted Dolly's. Exhaustion reflected in Dolly's eyes, though the woman seemed unaware as she rubbed at her cheeks and leant to press a palm atop her husband's hand.

"You and Ethel should go and enjoy yourselves. There will be plenty of time for us all later." She stood, and Ernest made to follow suit before the woman chuckled. "Really, Ernest. A day in bed is all I need. So much excitement over Ethel's arrival has left me ill prepared. I do feel terrible about it, but really, it's just a bit of fatigue." She glanced at Ethel, before looking at her husband. "I'm sure you two will make the day yours. There must be much for you to discuss and catch up on without myself there to interrupt two siblings reminiscing."

Ernest laughed and bowed his head, his concerns culled in the wake of his ardent wife. "Well, Ethel? What say *you*?"

Ethel paused and took her teacup. "Beulah can—"

"Go with you," Dolly replied, standing straight and cinching her robe. "I swear, if the woman stays here, I'll hear nothing but bickering from her and Aloysius all day, and then how shall I ever get to sleep? Besides, I have my own girl here for the day, and I'm sure Beulah would love to accompany you." She stooped, kissing Ernest upon his brow before taking a teacup and saucer to leave the room. "I only ask that when you return, do so with taffy. From the shop along the docks."

"Shirley's saltwater taffy shop?" Ernest said with a grin, following the footsteps of Dolly's departure with an affectionate eye.

"And make sure you get extra. You know how much I love it."

It was nice to see her brother laugh, though he had been no stranger to mirth before. Dolly's chipper demeanour was as catching as a cold, and even though the woman looked tired and poorly, Ethel couldn't help but sense a happy calm from her brother when the couple were in proximity to each other.

'Business often fouled a man', Ethel's mother had said once. It was the case of a good woman who kept the heads *and* hearts of their family and husbands secure at home. They were words Ethel vowed to live by if Roland hadn't died. But perhaps they were words still in need of abiding if a ghost was oppressing Eden Hall.

Ethel hoped a foreign bed was the result of all her troubles. As herself and Beulah donned their coats and pinned their hats in place, Ethel couldn't help but feel out of place in her blackened mourning clothes. She wanted to feel merry. The sun was bright and kissed her skin as they walked along the road, but adorned as such, her jolly feelings felt forced, as though contained within the barrier of her attire.

"You will have another dress by tomorrow, Miss Ethel." Beulah said, sensing her thoughts. Ethel smiled, glad for the woman's friendship.

"Thank you, Beulah. I don't know what I'd do without you."

Beulah laughed and fanned her fingers at her. "You'd do well enough, Miss Ethel. It just might take you a bit longer."

"Ethel was *always* one who had to ruminate a tad too long for my taste," Ernest chimed in, swinging a cane as they made their way to the boardwalk. "Always in her own head, you were, but I suppose patience is a virtue, even if it's not one of *mine*."

Beulah laughed. "*Absolutely* not, Mr. Arsenault. Remember when you stole that pie your mother made for church? Not only did you purloin it from the counter, but you tried to eat it before it cooled—dropped it— and burnt your mouth without managing a second bite."

The two laughed, but not without a shade of red spotting Ernest's cheeks.

"I'm not sure overthinking and patience are the same thing," Ethel said as she chuckled into her palm and nodded at a passing wagon. "But it's good fortune that someone like me keeps such boisterous company."

"Roland was always a quiet one as well, however," Ernest replied with a heartfelt sigh. "Together, you two were a library." He paused in his stride, waiting until Ethel stepped up next to him before wrapping his arm around her shoulders.

She thought he must be expecting her to frown, to confide in him her secret sorrows, but despite her loss, Ethel wished to linger in the pool of mirth that Ernest emitted. She smiled, hoping her eyes appeared earnest in their wish to move on from her bygone trauma.

"Am I a book then, brother? Or a librarian?"

Ernest reflected. His considering gaze looked alien upon his features as Ethel regretted, once again, the hue of her attire.

"I think, perhaps," he whispered, "that you are the library, and you're lost and dark and empty. However, Etty, there will come a day when you'll emerge from those shelves and open your doors to find many who love and wish to know you, and then *you'll* be the librarian."

"A poetic sentiment..." she mused, taken aback.

"I'd recommend letting family in first," he said, straightening as they turned to cross the boardwalk. "If you can care for family, abide us as we smear the ink and crinkle the pages of long forgotten tombs, then you'll be better equipped for callers and company."

Ethel laughed, listening as seagulls overhead cawed in unison. Offshore, spinning in the circles above the docks, a silver fish sparkled in the maws of a large albatross. "I *have* been thinking of letting go of the dark," she said, glancing towards her clothes.

Ernest regarded Beulah from over his shoulder. "Then let's go shopping! You've Dolly's gowns, but perhaps you can pick out a few of your own as well. Beulah has the better eye for clothes, but I'm more than happy to provide the pocketbook."

"You hear that, Miss Ethel? No more flour bag dresses for you."

"Nothing wrong with flour bags, Beulah. In fact, I've heard in Charlottetown, they've begun printing them with patterns for that very reason. But... I thought I'd like to spoil Ethel today. Yourself included, of course. Call it an apology for hard seats."

Beulah chortled, her round cheeks bright with the thought of a new, store-bought dress. Ethel could recall many times that Beulah and her mother would be outside, bleaching away the name of the flour companies from their cloth bags.

Five Roses or Gold Medal... Sugar sacks worked just as well.

"Throw in a few bags of that fancy Charlottetown flour, and I'll think about it, Mr. Arsenault."

Ernest shook his head but stepped ahead to lead the way. "You drive a hard bargain, Miss Murphy."

"And your man, Al, drives a *hard* stagecoach..."

* * *

The boardwalk had been a hub of activity. Shops and businesses along the roadside were buttressed with food vendors and performers. Steaming shellfish and fried potatoes perfumed the air, while the fragrance of the sea seasoned the dockyards spotted in the rusty sands brought forth from equine hooves. The Windmill restaurant spun in greeting, and the salt taffy shop with emerald shutters chimed hello to every visitor. They saw the Osbourne and St. Lawrence hotel's before catching a cab to Market Square to spend several hours at Linda's Fashion Frocks. Both women were tired after that, but excited for the boxes they were bringing home. Ernest had insisted on a slight detour to Hillsborough Square, though along the way they passed the Prince of Wales College.

"Does it have a library?" Ethel had asked, peering out the open carriage with wide eyes and fingers splayed along the edge of the stagecoach.

"No, but the honourable Thomas Dodd has promised us one." Ernest laughed.

It was about suppertime when they started home. Having stopped for a late lunch, the three of them weren't very hungry.

"I do hope Dolly has had something to eat," Ethel said for conversation. Beulah was next to Ethel, but the woman was half dozing and the heat of the sun had coloured the tip of her nose.

"If not," Beulah yawned, patting at Ethel's hand, "I can cook her a meal in the kitchens."

Ernest waved as the stagecoach stopped, and he hopped out to help the women disembark. "Her girl would have ensured she had eaten," he said, directing the driver to unload the boxes as he kicked the step and held open the door. "I'll have to work a tad late tonight," he said, holding out an arm to his sister. "Since there was a delay in my departure, there are a few bits of paperwork that have to be redone."

"Does that mean you're not staying, then?" Ethel asked, looking up at Eden Hall and thinking how large it seemed.

Ernest grinned and held out an arm for Beulah to disembark before turning and walking with Ethel towards the house. "Not for long, I'm afraid. I wanted to check in on Dolly before I headed out. I'm sure she will be eager to hear about what we got up to today."

Ethel tried to mirror his laugh, though in her heart she did not feel it. As darkness nestled among the briars surrounding Eden Hall, she wondered what night would bring, and if Dolly's illness was borne from the unsettled supernatural that meandered the halls and corridors.

Ethel hadn't been expecting Dolly awake, but as the doorknob was turned and the three of them wandered into the front foyer, the lady of the house was already descending the stairs. Her hair streamed around her shoulders, loosened like the white silk robe that hung about her frame like linens in a summer breeze. Though her face was flushed, it was but a subtle hue that danced along her nose and cheeks, while the pallor of her face and the bags beneath her eyes were gone.

"Ernest!" she greeted, a bouquet of silk gardenias in hand, "I had been waiting for you all to return. Did you have a lovely time?"

The two embraced, lost for moment in one another as Ethel struggled to control her expression. She was taken by surprise at the woman's demeanour. Not only did Dolly look revitalised, she looked even more youthful than yesterday, despite her unkempt hair and house attire. The fullness of her cheeks were emphasised by her bright and welcoming smile, and yet despite the warmth, Ethel was off put.

"Dolly, should you really be out of bed? You seemed so ill this morning."

Dolly smiled, the gesture reaching her eyes and causing a dimple to crease her left cheek. "I told you before it was just a restless sleep. I'm terribly sorry to have worried you."

"Have you eaten, Mrs. Arsenault?" Beulah asked, removing her coat to stand aside.

Dolly shook her head. "I've not. Though I have been hoping one of you remembered the taffy?" The hopeful gleam in the young lady's eye was not enough to quell the concern in her husband's.

"Did Adella-Ray not serve you supper?" he asked. Ethel supposed Ernest must have been referring to Dolly's housemaid, but as the younger woman shook her head, Ethel couldn't help but feel awkward in the midst of what appeared to be a pending argument.

"N-no. I sent her home early," Dolly replied, looking shamefaced as Ernest frowned. "I was just awful tired, and everything seemed to be a drum in my head. Really," she said, glancing around the room to include everyone in the exchange, "I'm all right now, though, if it isn't too much trouble, Miss Beulah, some toast and butter would be lovely."

Beulah nodded. "I'll send it up to your room," she said, already on her way towards the kitchens.

Ethel watched her go, then peered up towards the stairs where she knew her own bedchambers to be. "I think I'll change and make an early night of it. Your husband may be a marvellous tour guide, but he certainly wore me out."

Her brother chuckled, though it was obvious by his fleeting glance that he was grateful to be afforded a few moments alone with his wife. It was just as well. Ethel was feeling nervous, like rocks were settling in the pit of her stomach.

As she made her way upstairs and into her bedroom, she noticed her Gladstone bag sitting at the foot of the bed where she had last placed it. Her journal was inside, wrapped in potato cloth. A few old flowers, long crushed between the pages, tumbled out as she flipped through it. Poems, letters, stories she had written as a girl, were all contained within, as well as several crude drawings she remembered sketching at some point.

Portraits of her mother, her father, of Beulah and a few friends she'd once entertained, sat between the withered stems of carnations and lilacs. Her brother as a boy, Roland, and of the tall ship that had set sail with him upon it...

Ethel recalled how excited she was on that day. Roland had family in New Brunswick, and he and her father had set sail to tell them of the engagement. She remembered waving them goodbye, wishing, despite propriety, that she could have sent Roland off with a kiss. Her father hadn't been sick then, but he had developed tuberculosis shortly thereafter. The doctors thought it had been contracted on the boat, and he had to be kept in New Brunswick until they determined it was of the spine and not contagious. Roland had been on his way back with news of her father's illness. Then, he went missing at sea.

Ethel turned the page, eyes settling on faded blood. Like the darkened petals of an old, crushed rose, it was splayed in four thick slashes along the left side of the book, slid across the paper, and stopped short of the right page margin. Two pictures had been scrawled over top, but Ethel closed the journal to escape them before they could take shape in her mind.

She wished she had photographs of them all, but most of her drawings had been made after her family had already passed. Even the portrait of Ernest was of him as a boy, before he'd moved away and married Dolly.

"People need to be alive to take a photograph," Ethel mused, shoving her journal back inside her Gladstone bag. She had only seen a handful of them. Gray, still images upon a shiny stamp of paper. She wondered if Dolly had ever had one done. If Ernest had.

She sighed, laying back upon the bed to stare up into the darkness of its canopy. Today had been a fun day, not one she ought to come home from to wallow in residual melancholy. She decided to change, then go down in the den to read for awhile. Perhaps she could check in on Fritz and Mr. Carlow in the stables. Aloysius seemed of a jovial sport, full of stories and adventures.

It was after suppertime when Ethel came downstairs. Beulah was puttering around Ernest's study, dusting and arranging several quills that had been left to dry on his desk.

"You'd think he was your father with how he keeps a mess," she said. There was a teacup on the mantelpiece, alongside an open bottle of gin that Ethel recognized from the kitchens. The wastebasket over by his chair was full of old papers and documents, balled into bundles. "I mean, look at the fingerprints here! If Old Master Arsenault *knew* in what condition his guns were being stored..."

"I was thinking of heading outside to speak with Mr. Carlow and Mr. Humphry," Ethel said, watching as Beulah scrubbed at the glass with a damp rag. Ethel figured Ernie must have left the house already, else he probably would have shooed them both away. If he kept a study like his father,

Ernest probably didn't like anyone tidying it up either.

"That scoundrel?" Beulah replied, standing and wiping at her brow. "Surely you must be speaking of Mr. Carlow, because we both know Fritz Humphrey is good for nary a sentence."

"The way you tut about him makes me think you fancy him, Beulah." Ethel hid her grin behind her hand, watching as the flush on Beulah's cheeks spread like a bushfire to her eyebrows.

"You best get those thoughts well out of your head, Miss Arsenault."

Ethel laughed at the nerve she'd ignited. She'd known Beulah since they were both children, and Beulah only ever addressed her as such when she was cross. "How can I, when you are blushing so?"

"I am not!" Beulah cried, tossing the rag on the desk and managing her way into the front hall.

Ethel followed her out, watching how the older woman made hammers of her fists in mock offence. "Does that mean you won't accompany me, then?"

Beulah was already grabbing her shawl and passed another to Ethel as she donned it. "Well, I can't have you alone with him. He's bound to tell you some God-awful story that a lady has no mind to hear..."

"Absolutely." Ethel nodded.

"And a man with a head full of rocks is bound to need a load of sand to fill the gaps."

Ethel laughed, unsure of the metaphor Beulah was trying to conjure. "Well then, lead the way, Miss Murphy."

"I shall!"

Chapter 6

The evening had been comely, with the two men happy to entertain the pair of obliging women. Though Fritz said very little, his face alone harkened back to Green's Shore, which offered Ethel an odd source of contentment. Aloysius and Beulah bickered like age old friends, while moths fluttered amongst the kerosene lanterns, and the horses whinnied and swatted at the occasional fly that wandered up their flanks.

"It's nice to have you two here," Al said before taking a hearty pull from his flask. "The Hall can be a lonely thing when Mr. Arsenault's away, and though it's new, it creaks and groans like an old girl."

"I'm a tad surprised they haven't hired a butler," Beulah said, leaning back on a wicker rocking chair as Fritz blew a puff of smoke to waft out from the barn. "With a household as large as Eden Hall, it's unfathomable to think the lady should do it all herself."

Al shrugged and scratched the nape of his neck. "The servants during the day make do, and Mr. Arsenault takes care of our wages well in advance."

"Have you ever heard the house at night, Mr. Carlow? Groan or… creak, I mean?"

Beulah frowned and made a curt noise of disapproval at Ethel's question. Aloysius smiled, leaning forward with a glance at Fritz, who sat with his back against the stable door and his feet upon a stool.

"Stories," the old man said, his cap tipped down over his eyes and his pipe but a twig amidst the brambles of his coarse, curly beard. "Always one for stories, Ethel is."

"That right?" Al replied, rubbing at the sides of his mouth to smooth the hint of beard that had been sprouting. "Well, I suppose I can't say I've personally experienced anything supernatural, but I've heard stories from the maids."

"A hobby of yours, it seems," Beulah muttered with a glance sideways. "If only you worked as much as you prattled on."

Aloysius laughed but said nothing to further fuel the ornery Beulah Murphy. "Eden Hall is young," he began, looking up at Ethel as his arms dangled across his knees and his hands clasped the flask of gin. "It was commissioned by your father, as you know, but though it's new, its bones are old."

"How so?" Ethel asked, her heartbeat beginning to race.

"The wood that was used to build it came from a shipyard, and the story goes that some of the lumber was from a vessel that had crashed when Point Prim lighthouse was out of commission."

Beulah turned back, the creak of her chair the only indication that she had been listening. "I'm not sure this story is—"

Ethel shook her head. "No. I want to hear it, Beulah"

Al nodded. Beulah was silent.

Ethel gestured for him to continue.

"Well, as the girls inside told it, there was a sailor 'board the ship that perished, but his body was never found. I've heard rumour that it was the captain of the ship, which is why Eden Hall is disturbed some nights with whispers and groans."

"You think he haunts the Hall?"

"Ethel, that's silly..."

Aloysius leant back, swatting at a moth that was drawn to a lantern overhead. "Not sure," he shrugged. "Though the maids thought so. We don't like to say too much about it, what with Miss Dolly being alone here all the time, but she's never mentioned anything, and it makes for a good bedtime story."

"Probably because it's all foolish." Beulah interrupted, standing and correcting her skirts before turning towards the house. "Nothing but a foolish yarn to disrupt your dreams, Miss Ethel."

Aloysius chuckled, watching as the serving woman ushered Ethel from her seat.

"Had no mind to scare you, Miss Murphy. If you find yourself a fright, I'll fight off the phantoms for ya. Me and Fritz'll be out here all night with the horses if you get afraid."

Fritz was already dozing with his head tucked back and eyes closed beneath his cap. Ethel didn't think Fritz would be much for warding off ghosts, but despite the fears budding in her chest, she watched and smiled as a crimson hue filled Beulah's cheeks.

"Let's go, Miss Ethel," Beulah said with a shake of her head, as though it was enough to ward off her abashment. "We've spent more than enough time with this scoundrel as it is."

Ethel could hear the deception in Beulah's words, and she thought Mr. Carlow could as well, because he laughed and offered a liquor salute at their departure. Ethel could sense a growing fondness between them despite their bickering but didn't pull away as Beulah led them both back towards the house.

"Pay no mind to them. Too much gin and whiskey."

The house was dark when they entered the foyer, and even the stained-glass windows that framed the doors were unable to shed any moonlight onto the oaken floor and sycamore staircase that led upstairs.

"I left the lamp in the stables," Ethel admitted, looking up at the gas piping along the ceiling. She thought about lighting the chandelier, but figured the glow would disturb Dolly who was probably already abed. "Should we go and retrieve it?"

Beulah shook her head. "I've no wish to go back to the stables and smell the horses. Just hang on to me," she chuckled, "surely together we can fumble our way upstairs."

They had made the first landing with minimal effort, though the width of Miss Beulah's hips had caused Ethel to knock the side of the banister more than once. Both women were trying to be quiet, though the creaking of the stairs and the fumbling of their skirts hailed their way like a town crier. They hadn't yet reached the second floor when Ethel paused, shot through the belly with fear.

A shadow the size of a man stood like a tomb at the top of the stairs. Watching them. Its appearance was followed by a woman's voice. "W-who—Ernest?!"

Beulah nearly toppled and would have fallen if not for Ethel's tenuous hold. All three women shrieked in unison, their shouts enough to rattle the windows before silence filled the hall.

Dolly was before them, dressed in a robe, her hair askew. Her eyes were wide, and just barely perceptible as she caught her breath and wandered down a single stair to confront them.

"Ethel? Beulah! What are you doing this time of night?"

Ethel was holding her chest and ignoring the litany of Irish curses that were being whispered by the woman beside her. "Dolly! We're—I thought you were..." Ethel let out a laugh of relief. "I'm sorry. We were outside with Fritz and Al. I forgot the lantern."

"If I were an older woman, I'd need a new pair of bloomers," Beulah huffed, marching onward as Dolly let the two women pass onto the second floor hall. They could faintly see the candlelight pouring from the stairs leading up towards the third floor bedroom, and Dolly's heaving bosom.

"I thought you were a burglar!" she hollered.

"I'm so sorry, Dolly. We didn't mean to wake you. We were trying to be quiet—" A scuttle from upstairs caused her to pause, and Ethel glanced towards the stairs and master bedroom above.

"Is—"

Dolly pursed her lips, folding her arms and wrapping her robe tighter as she glanced over one shoulder. "It's just Ernest. I didn't want to wake him." She turned her head toward the master bedroom and said, "Go to sleep, Darling, it's only Ethel and Beulah!"

"When did he get back? I didn't hear a carriage ride up," Beulah asked before Ethel could.

"A little while ago. He's had... a bit to drink, so..."

"So, he sent his wife down to check for a burglar?"

Dolly blinked, unaccustomed to being questioned so bluntly by a maid. The older woman however, looked more offended on Dolly's behalf as she stared daggers up towards the staircase. Seeming to sense this, Mrs. Arsenault held up her hands, and smiled to diffuse the tension. "He's overly tired, is all. Carousing is a part of business, and he's been up to his ears in it for the last few days. The gin has gotten the better of him."

"Well, you are sick as well."

"I'm feeling much better, though I think a good night's rest would warrant a happier day come tomorrow."

Ethel nodded and made sure to squeeze Beulah's arm as she tugged her towards their chambers. "For all of us, I think. We are sorry to disturb you, Dolly. Have a good night?"

"I shall. Goodnight, ladies. Sleep well."

"Sleep well," Ethel agreed as she crept down the hall to her room. She felt a cramping in her stomach, and a rush between her legs as she parted ways with Beulah and sat upon her bed. Her mirth was gone and Ethel winced at the pain of her monthly cycle before pressing her palms to the flat plane of her stomach. The stories of the shipyard captain fed her thoughts, as well as the phantom of a man she swore she'd seen atop the stairs.

Was he watching her, even after she changed and went to bed? In the drape of the curtains and from the shadows on the wall and floor, she saw him. Then she heard more thumps from upstairs as though within the house itself he dwelt.

She fell asleep to the sound of scratching, like a bough upon the door...

Chapter 7

The days were dandelions, sprouting and flourishing and wafting away in puffs to seed more weeds anew. Though the roads had been muck-filled and swampy when they'd arrived, gradually they were becoming less burdensome and easier to promenade when the days were hot. Ernest's trip had been postponed, but that meant he spent the days at work, oftentimes taking a break to show Ethel the delights of Queen's Square and Victoria Row or holed up in his study pouring over papers and the occasional glass of gin.

Ethel was enjoying her days at Eden Hall, wandering outside in the small gardens, or taking a stagecoach in town with Miss Murphy to appraise the daily catch and supply of vegetables hauled in from the neighbouring farms. Though the nights were seldom peaceful, Ethel had resolved to keep her concerns private. No one else in the house seemed bothered or affected, so she often napped during the afternoon, dozing after writing in her journal or upon finishing a few chapters of Little Women.

"I'm certain there must be something in the attic," Ernest grumbled at breakfast one morning. His departure had been finalised for the next day and a few men had been around to load up a few personal effects he had packed for the voyage. It was a beautiful midweek morning, and the windows in the dining room had been removed to let in the scent of grass and sunshine.

Dolly was sitting opposite her husband at the little breakfast table, while Ethel was in the middle. Both women looked up from their plates to regard Ernest as he poured a fresh cup of tea for himself.

"Adella-Ray, will you not check the liquor cabinet in the study for a bottle of the blueberry spirits? There's a touch of maple in it that I'm sure will stir the tongues of the Americans."

The serving woman was in the foyer, handing an order for milk to the carrier before she turned towards the study as asked.

"The attic?" Dolly piped up, directing the conversation backwards. She was picking around the sauce of her eggs benedict, combing it over the white poached pillow like a toupée on a bald man's head. "Is there something up there that you forgot to pack?"

Ernest shook his head. "No, but I think an animal has gotten up there somehow. I've been hearing it scuttling around the last few nights." He looked up and smiled, as though to excuse his ramblings. "I'll ask Al to take a look. I don't want it scaring you ladies while I'm gone for work."

"An animal? Like a racoon?" Ethel pursed her lip, wondering if all this time she had been hearing a poor frightened animal in the walls, rather than the lost soul of a sea captain. Since Al had told his story a few nights ago, Ethel was certain no one besides herself had heard anything of the sort.

Ernest bent to sip his tea before spooning a few generous lumps of sugar to dissolve within the amber fluid. "Something like that," he said. "I've heard it a few times recently, mostly at night, so it must be some kind of nocturnal creature."

"I've not heard a thing! Have you, Ethel?" Dolly asked, her fingers pressing at the hollow of her throat.

Ethel frowned, wondering whether she ought to say anything. "It's an unfamiliar house..." she'd decided, "so I'm afraid even normal sounds would feel foreign to me."

"I'm sure it's just—"

"Sorry to disrupt, Mr. Arsenault," Adella-Ray said from the wide open French doors that bisected the breakfast area from the foyer, "but I'm afraid I am unable to locate your spirits."

Ernest swivelled in his chair to face the exit. "Did you check the cabinet in the study? I know I put a bottle in there a few weeks ago."

Adella-Ray nodded, a few mouse-brown strands of hair bobbing out the borders of her maid cap. "I remember, Sir. But it seems it's gone."

Dolly laughed, finally pausing to take her first bite of breakfast. "You probably drank it, Ernie. Perhaps without thinking? You've been working late all week, seldom even coming home till morning."

Ernest harrumphed, though he only seemed mildly perplexed as he turned to resume his position at the table. "Perhaps so, Darling," he said in a tone unconvinced at the suggestion. "Though I was sure—I don't care much for the stuff. Too fruity..." He scratched his head, "I suppose I'll have to buy another before I go." He wiped his chin, smoothing out the corners of his moustache before standing up to excuse himself.

"Just another thing to add to the list," he said. "I won't be able to keep you company today, I'm afraid." He looked at his pocket watch. "Too much to do before departure tomorrow. Will you two be all right while I'm gone?"

Ethel smiled, while Dolly offered a confident wave of her hand. "We'll find something to occupy us."

"The day is lovely, after all," Ethel agreed.

Ernest nodded. "Very well," he said before turning towards the foyer where Adella-Ray had already fetched his hat and coat. "I won't be home till late. So be sure to dine without me."

Ethel thought her brother must be looking forward to the voyage, if only to relax. She'd hardly seen him rest while at home and hoped he'd have a short respite from the plethora of business affairs he was embroiled in while sailing to Boston. *She* would never have been able to rest inside the belly of a boat, though Ethel knew, like Roland and their father, Ernest adored the sea.

"Do you think you'd fancy a trip out today, Dolly?" Ethel asked when they'd been left alone. Dolly was stirring a bit of milk into her tea, looking far away and transfixed. She almost tipped the cup over when she realised she was being addressed.

"Oh! Sorry, Etty. My mind went wandering," Dolly said, grabbing a napkin to dab at a few spots that had soaked into the tablecloth.

Ethel couldn't help but notice the few dark lines pulling at the corners of Dolly's cheeks. "Have you been sleeping soundly?" she asked, wondering if the noise at night was more conspicuous than Dolly had led on. A part of Ethel wished it were so, if only to talk with someone else about it.

"Well... no. Not really," Dolly replied, "To be sure, I—" She looked around, then gazed out towards the road from the open windows. "I don't want to worry you, but... Have you heard anything from the attic, Ethel? Something like... an animal?"

Ethel paused and pursed her lips. She was at odds as to whether she should say anything, especially on the eve of Ernest's departure. "I—"

"You have, haven't you?"

Ethel went quiet, knowing her face was giving her away.

Dolly sighed. "I think perhaps I've been sleepwalking," she said, looking down at her cup of tea and blinking as if to hold back tears. "I don't want to trouble Ernest with it, but I've found myself sometimes in the hall or wandering downstairs. I've noticed things are moved at times and can only conclude that I've moved them."

Ethel had also noticed things put aside in strange ways. A cup on a bookshelf, a pipe in the pantry, a common room locked when there was no one inside it. But could it be that Dolly was walking about asleep?

Again, the lady of Eden Hall sighed, and then stood up from the table. "Don't trouble Al with the attic. I'll speak with him, but then I'll probably head to bed. You should take dear Beulah and go out and enjoy the day."

"If you're sleepwalking, you really ought to tell Ernie. What if you fall? What if you hurt yourself?" Ethel grasped Dolly's hand, speaking past the fog of her thoughts. A story of a sailor had been enough to spook her, enough to colour Ethel's suspicions and proffer doubt in the face of Dolly's explanation, but the fear of the poor woman falling took precedence.

"I don't want to worry him. Especially when he's leaving tomorrow." Dolly smiled and looked away towards the foyer. "Maybe I can lock my door and drink a hefty glass of gin before bed." She laughed as she gave Ethel's hand a squeeze and then stooped to retake her chair. "When you get back, we both can. We'll drink until we can do nothing but dream."

"I'm not much of a drinker," Ethel admitted, trying not to sound dour.

"All the better! Because I'm certain Ernie's done away with most and packed away the rest."

"I could pick some up—"

Dolly nodded and sprang up like a daisy despite her fatigue. "Great. And include taffy from Shirley's and chocolate from Miss Laura's. Enough for me, and you and Beulah."

Ethel nodded and watched after Dolly as she sauntered up the stairs. She thought the idea that Dolly was sleepwalking should provide a relief of some sort, but in fact, Ethel was puzzled. Exiting the breakfast nook, Ethel wandered outside where she knew Beulah would be arranging for transport to town. She smiled at the sight of her homemaker laughing at something Aloysius had said and determined to keep her mind on the day and the delight she wished to derive from it.

They left together shortly before mid-morning, stopping first to retrieve the few treats that Dolly had requested for later that evening. Though the mud had been fierce during their first promenade into Charlottetown, it had died up over the last several days due to the fond weather. Large ruts caused the carriage to bounce and rock, so the two ladies had Al drop them off at the corner of Queen's and Saint George street before their little excursion could take a toll on their backsides. Here, hemlock planks had been laid over the dried dust and dirt of the city's streets, and walking along, the two women perused the wares of the downtown warren.

Shops selling boots were plentiful, and Ethel supposed the reason for this was due to the terrible condition of the roads. They wandered into a few shops selling books and stopped at E.W. Taylor's jewellery store to find a gift for Dolly.

"Something to grant a bit of cheer," Ethel explained as she walked into the small front room of the store's parlour. Shelves and open cabinets lined each wall and were filled with clocks, silverware, and sparkling baubles meant to catch the eye. A few men were inside, looking over a selection of spectacles displayed in an ornate glass counter, while a sweet young couple whispered over an array of rings.

"What kind of trim do you reckon Dolly would like?" Beulah asked, following Ethel's gaze as it swept over the myriad of different items.

"Something bright. Something... lovely."

Beulah snorted at the response.

Ethel couldn't blame her. Everything here was lovely, and certainly everything sparkled. "Look, Beulah. This brooch looks just like the one Dolly has." The sight of the familiar pin was cause enough for Ethel to believe she was in the right place. "Perhaps she'd like another one." A matching set of silver swallows inset with lazuli gemstones sat in a box beside it, and Ethel's smile grew. "I'd like to purchase these, please," she said, waving at the clerk while Beulah leant to look.

"Are you thinking of gifting both to her?" she asked.

Ethel shook her head. "One to Ernest and one to Dolly. A memento of each other to keep them connected, even while they're away from one another."

"A sweet sentiment from a hopeless romantic." Beulah snickered, covering her laugh with the back of her hand.

"Hardly hopeless!" Ethel replied, swatting at the woman as she took out her pocketbook.

"Are you reading that romance book again?"

Ethel paused, mouth agape as she glared needles at Miss Beulah Murphy. "Little Women is *not* a romance!" she began, pausing as the clerk beside them turned to look in their direction.

"Excuse me, ladies," he interjected. "I have a gent here that would benefit from the advice of the fairer sex. Would you, while I finish with this other customer?"

Ethel nodded, turning as the clerk departed to regard a gentleman who had his cap in hand. He was a young man, dressed in dirty trousers with an elegant frock coat that was a size too large for him. The quality of the roads must have struck its mark on his pant cuffs.

"Sorry to bother you," he said, looking askance with red ears.

Ethel noticed that the man's suspenders were showing beneath his coat. She smiled. "How can I help you, Sir?"

"I'm looking for a gift. F-for someone special. These two things are all they have within my budget, but... I can't decide."

Ethel looked at the two sets of earrings laid out upon the glass countertop, careful not to pay mind to the woeful tone of the young man's voice. One was a set of silver clusters dangling with polished glass, the other, seed pearl teardrops.

"Both are lovely," Ethel encouraged. "May I ask what the occasion is?"

He was looking at his feet and pressed his lips into a thin line. "She just deserves them, is all. She deserves the world, but... It's beyond my means."

Beulah sighed. "Every foolish young man in love wants to give their sweetheart the world, but they never realise the world isn't theirs to give."

"Oh hush, Beulah," Ethel tutted with a smile, waving the woman away. "You're ruining the sentiment." She leant forward as a way to place a barrier between the young man and her serving girl. "To be honest, Sir, I don't think I ought to decide for you. If I do, the gift won't really be yours, would it? But I can offer a bit of advice. Whatever pair you choose, she is sure to wear them often and with a smile on her face. She will think of you whenever she dons them, and whenever they manage to caress her jaw. Because of this, they should be symbolic of you and yours, and though they may not be the world you'd like to give her, taking the time to decide will mean the world to her."

The young man was quiet, his face a portrait of thought as Ethel moved to pay the clerk and wait for her gift to be packaged. She watched as the man stared at the countertop, not at the twin set of earrings but seemingly at his own reflection.

"Thank you," he said after a time, as the two women were heading out. He had green eyes, like the sea, a wide nose and boyish cheeks that leant youth to a slim and cleft chin.

"You're welcome, Sir. Goodluck!" she called as they walked back through the door to the outside. The sea air was vibrant in Ethel's nose and her bags were already heavy on each arm.

"Should we head back, Beulah?" she asked, feeling in high spirits.

"Yes, please, Miss Ethel. Those clouds over there are looking dark, and I wouldn't want to be waltzing around this bog when it's wet."

"A rainy night for reading," Ethel mused, as they wandered back down from Queen's Street to where they knew Mr. Carlow was waiting for them.

Chapter 8

Ethel had only managed four chapters of her book before she succumbed to sleep, and if she hadn't have read the book several times before, she was certain she wouldn't have remembered anything of the story after retiring to her room that night.

True to her word, Dolly had insisted they all stay up together, until Beulah begged to be released at seven and Ethel feigned exhaustion at ten. Together, the two sisters finished off three bottles of wine, and a few spirits that Dolly had concocted in the kitchens. Never one for a hearty drink, Ethel had resorted to Dolly's arm as they both clambered up the stairs to bed. The echoes of their laughter reverberated in Ethel's dreams, tied in her subconscious like a letter in a bottle at the bottom of the sea. Faces of men and women she had seen throughout the day danced in tandem to the lofting murk of slumber.

She couldn't remember getting to bed but recalled the tug of ribbons around her waist, and the feel of swollen feet being released from the leather confines of laced up boots. The only reason Ethel knew that she had read four chapters of her book was because that was where the spine was halved upon the floor when she picked up again.

"Oh God. Miss Ethel, tell me you're all right! Please?"

The cool press of a woman's palm caused her eyes to open, and though the house seemed warm, Ethel felt as moist as kelp at the conclusion of a particularly high tide. She rubbed at her eyes, the sparks of a headache flaring behind her eyelids. Though her boots were off, and her corset unlaced beneath her camisole, she was still half dressed. She laid upon the made but wrinkled covers of her four poster bed.

"Beulah?" Ethel could hardly recognize her own voice. "Goodness, my mouth is dry. Might I bother you for a cup of water?" She watched the plump woman glance sidelong towards the end table next to the bed. The curtains had not been drawn, and the first threads of sunrise filtered in through the windows of the Queen Anne's turret like blades. Ethel looked away, wishing she had closed the bed's canopy drapes.

"I-I think we ought to go downstairs." Beulah sniffed, obvious relief painting her features as she pressed a thumb and pointer to her forehead. She turned away, rubbing at her eyes with a cloth. "I thought... I had such a hard time waking you, that I thought..."

Ethel winced, fighting against the pain in her head until she was able to sit up upon the bed. "Beulah?" There was an ache in her chest, and a pepper of phantom fingertips were tracing circles along her spine. "What is going on?"

It wasn't like Beulah to be quiet, but in the ensuing silence, Ethel heard voices bouncing up the stairs from the foyer in boisterous commotion. Footfalls that felt as though they'd rupture walls and send the rooftop tumbling down were followed by the gonging of the grandfather clock in the hall. Ethel only heard it ring three times before Beulah interrupted its toll.

"Ernest has been murdered, Miss Ethel. Last night. Right in the hall outside our rooms." Information was gargled behind the static of sobs and laboured breathing. Fumbling for purchase, Ethel grasped at words.

"W-what?"

"He was... m-murdered!"

The thump in Ethel's chest took her breath away. Her soul departed to search the corridors of existence for reality—a *right* reality: one that was kind and good and happy. But the terrible truth chimed like the hour on the grandfather clock and her soul returned with the cruel dawning of verity.

"Ernie is..." Ethel's lungs deflated, and with only extreme effort did she manage to draw in breath. It pained her. "How? Why, Beulah?"

The woman shook her head. "They think it was a burglar, but... Oh Miss Ethel, I thought you'd been poisoned when you didn't wake up. I thought something terrible..." Beulah's eyes were red and welling like wounds. Not only for the benefit of the sobbing woman, but in an effort to hold herself together, Ethel reached forwards to embrace her friend. Her fingers pressed into the pliant flesh of Beulah's shoulders and anchored there, until a knock on the door forced her away.

She was shattered, but at the noise, Ethel found the strength to hold the shards together.

"Miss Arsenault?" Ethel glanced up at Constable Andrew Bertram who looked like an ageing portrait framed in the doorway. No longer adorned in a suit smelling of dust, his officers uniform made him look grim, official. Like the reaper at work. "I'm sorry to interrupt, but if you could join us downstairs, Miss Arsenault, we have a few questions."

"For the Lord's sake! Can't you give her a mom—"

"Where's Dolly?" Ethel asked, looking wide-eyed between Miss Murphy and Constable Bertram. Beulah had reached her hand between them to grasp at Ethel's fingers. For that, Ethel was glad. She had been shaking.

"She's downstairs," he replied, turning away to offer her a moment of privacy. Though still clothed, her shirtwaist was untucked, and her clothing creased from sleep. "Please join her when you're ready—"

"Constable Bertram!"

He paused in the doorway, looking sidelong towards the floorboards.

"W-where is my brother now? He's not—"

She could see his lips press into a thin line as she struggled to conclude her enquiry. Thankfully, he didn't wait for her to utter it.

"They've taken him already, but there are officers in the hall. You should prepare yourself, Miss Arsenault." He pulled the brim of his hat down across his brow as he left, his departure leaving the door to creak closed.

Ethel stood from the bed, lurching towards the vanity to right her appearance. Her hair was unkempt and loosened from its pins, but more bother was the unbound corset floating beneath her clothes.

"Miss Ethel. Should you really—"

Ethel spun around, her face a startled mix of terror and determination. "Please help me with this, Beulah."

"But—"

Ethel shook her head, her glassy eyes swollen with tears that she was trying to hold back. "We can't leave Dolly alone down there. She's lost her husband, she's—" She turned again, forcing her eyes agape to keep them from shedding. Ethel knew what it was like to lose a husband, even if she had never been married.

Pressing at her skirts, the thought of having to wear black again came unbidden as she contemplated its blue lace, and Ethel, pooling on the floor, gasped as her sorrow cut blades into her heart and blinded her.

* * *

"Why are you doing this to me?" Dolly's voice sounded muffled behind a crushed handkerchief as she wept. "Must I live out what happened over and over again? It was awful! I—I can hardly bear it!"

Ethel's anxieties welled inside her chest like a blister about to burst. As she walked from the bottom step of the foyer into the sitting room, she watched as Dolly sat upon the sofa. Her shoulders quaked as she floundered in a fit of sobs. A police deputy was standing before her, an open notepad in his right hand as he looked down at the young woman with an apologetic frown.

Bertram was trailing behind Ethel from the upper landing, and Beulah after that, held up by the vivid, white, linen blanket that had been thrown over Ernest's dead body. Ethel had refrained from looking and was glad the constable had stood as a barrier from the horrific crime scene, but the images in her periphery haunted her, seared forever in her living memory.

Meeting the gaze of her sobbing sister-in-law, Ethel ran past the open doors of the sitting room, calling out as Dolly held open her arms.

96

"We just need to make sure we have all the details written down, Ma'am," the officer replied, taking a step back as Andrew Bertram entered. "The quicker we can identify the intruder, the quicker we can bring him to justice."

Ethel held the young woman, pulling Dolly's open robe closed and cradling her close. There were constables everywhere, looking about the house, glancing at the pair of women with pity in their eyes. Ethel recalled the stoic empathy from onlookers, of officers hardened to death when Roland died. Andrew Bertram had that look now, of duty and obligation in the face of tragedy. He asked if he could take the notebook.

"Ethel, I am so sorry. It all happened so fast and I couldn't do anything about it."

"W-what happened, Dolly?"

The other officer left, and Constable Bertram extracted a lead pencil from his breast pocket to scrawl down notes. Feeling ill at ease to be used in such a way, Ethel tried to ignore him, focusing instead on the words pouring from Dolly's mouth.

"I-I think it was a burglar! I heard a noise and saw Ernest wrestling with a man in the hall. It was dark. I couldn't see. I heard the gun go off and—and... Ernie fell!"

"Do you know how the intruder got into the house?" Constable Bertram asked, his features softening as the two women turned to regard him.

Dolly shook her head. "I—I don't know. I was in the bedroom sleeping when I heard a struggle outside the door."

"You said before that Mr. Arsenault had come home late."

Dolly nodded, caught in a fit of sobs. "He was supposed to leave for a business trip tomorrow."

Ethel cradled her tighter, held hostage by a maternal sense of responsibility. *How did I not hear anything? Especially the sound of a gunshot?*

"Do you recall how tall the assailant was? Any little details would help greatly, Mrs. Arsenault."

Dolly shook her head, wiping at her eyes. "He was smaller than Ernie. Slimmer, but perhaps of a similar height."

"And you didn't hear anything, Miss Ethel?"

Ethel looked up. Her confusion reflected in Bertram's brown eyes. "I-I didn't. No."

"I could hardly wake her, Constable. I thought perhaps she'd been hurt or poisoned."

They all three glanced towards the doorway, watching as Beulah Murphy wrung her skirts and tried in vain to stifle her weeping. Next to her was Dolly's maid, Adella-Ray. Ethel wondered when the girl had arrived, or if she'd been here the whole time.

Bertram stood. "Miss Murphy, was it? What about you? Did you hear anything of the sort?"

"I—" Ethel blanched at the worried look on Beulah's face as it was shot in her direction. Bertram sighed and lowered his notebook as Miss Murphy stumbled to reply.

"The investigation will take awhile. I'm afraid you won't be able to stay here," he said, turning on his heel to address the lady of the hall. "Is there anywhere else close by that you can stay?"

"F-for how long?" Dolly replied, looking up towards the second floor. "I suppose we could stay at The Pavillion on—on Great George Street."

"Good. I'll have one of the other constables run over and tell them to prepare some rooms." He turned, "You said you were her maid? She'll need to pack and change."

Adella-Ray nodded with a curtsy as she spanned the short distance between herself and Dolly. Receiving the lady with a delicate touch, Ethel watched the two women leave the room before her attention was called back to Bertram.

"Miss Murphy," he said again with a gesture to the sofa. "If you would please elaborate on what you saw? Heard?"

Ethel shifted to allow Beulah to sit, and she did so with slight hesitation.

"I wasn't home last night. The stable hand—Mr. Carlow, invited me to a dance down on Richmond Street."

Ethel smiled with watery eyes at the flush that blossomed on Beulah's cheeks. Taking the woman by the hand, Ethel embraced her, glad that she had been away enjoying herself, yet sad that she'd returned to such tragedy.

"We didn't get home until very early this morning. Al came in, saw Mrs. Arsenault sobbing, and ran to get the constable. I stayed with her downstairs until Adella came. We all were too scared to go upstairs where the body was, and I didn't dare go check on Ethel until you all arrived. I am so glad you're all right, Miss Ethel."

"And you heard nothing of what happened?" Constable Bertram asked, his eyes curious as he glanced at Ethel.

"Dolly and I—We were up late last night. We were enjoying a few libations. Dolly has been having trouble sleeping, so we thought the alcohol may help."

"Trouble sleeping? Can you elaborate, Miss Arsenault?"

Ethel bit her bottom lip. "She's been sleepwalking and waking up in different areas of the house. She was... embarrassed, and didn't want to worry Ernie, especially on the eve of his trip, so... We drank a lot and—" She covered her mouth with her hand, disgusted that she may have slept through her own brother's murder. Could she have done anything if she had been awake? How long did he suffer? How long did he lay there, warmed by the pool of his own lifeblood?

Constable Bertram paused and stooped to regard her. Ethel was dazed by the pity in his eyes, and the subtle empathy that poured from the youthful features so earnestly hidden behind a stoic moustache. Lowering her hand, she leant back, if only to ensure the distance between them remained appropriate. He followed her however, inhaling as if to prolong the proximity.

"My condolences to you, Miss. Arsenault," he said after a while. "Your brother was an affluent man and will be sorely missed by the community of Charlottetown. I assure you, we will do everything in our power to find the culprit, but it may take awhile."

Awhile. Ethel had heard that word before. They had said it when they were searching for Roland's body. Awhile, as it turned out, could also mean endlessly.

"May I call upon you later, Miss?"

Ethel sniffed and wondered if her thoughts were reflected in her face because Bertram stood up and looked askance. "Of course," she said, her words drawing his face back down to regard her. "And please," Ethel continued, taking him by the hand, "If you find anything out, anything at all, please let me know. I... I don't want to be left in the dark."

He gave her hand a squeeze and nodded, smiling, though the expression failed to reach his eyes. She watched him walk away, towards Ernest's den to speak to another officer. She wondered what was to become of them all now. Ernie had been the patriarch, the head of the entire Arsenault family. Now all that was left was his sister. His poor, thin, quiet, awkward sister. All Ethel desired to do was sob in the arms of another. So, she did just that, and Beulah—ever her most dearest friend—sobbed with her.

Chapter 9

Ethel sat in the eye of an auric room, acacia wood polished and gleaming around the four poster bed. Ethel was alone, her clothes rumpled and damp from where Dolly had sobbed upon her breast for hours. Outside the room, the halls of the Pavillion were quiet but for the soft breeze that was sometimes let in through the windows at the far end. Tomorrow, Ethel thought, she'd have to unpack her black gowns and put away the newly bought items Ernest had so generously gifted to her. Ethel was loath to look at them, despite the comfort she had once derived from the mundane articles a few days prior. Their meaning was foul now, a reminder of the death she'd outlived and how she was now the sole survivor of the Arsenault family line.

Alone: its meaning was an abyss that would pull her down to an early grave, and yet, as Ethel sat upon the bed, she wondered how the darkness would taste, and if there'd be a hidden light at the deepest depths of her depression.

"I'm so tired," Dolly interrupted, entering the bedchamber from the adjoining den located on the far wall. The new widow was in her evening attire, and the cotton gown hung around her ankles and caught the light to reveal her silhouette. Darkened crescents hung like macabre smiles from Dolly's eyes. They dangled upon her cheeks and drug her lips towards her chin to be framed in black trenches. Still, Dolly looked beautiful.

"I'm sorry, Etty. This must be so hard on you. I never thought..." Dolly sat upon the bed and blinked in an effort to keep the tears from falling down her cheeks. Her hands were knotting in her lap, as though to ward away the sorrow she carried so she may offer comfort in its stead. "I didn't think, ever, that something like this would happ—"

Ethel shushed her and grabbed Dolly about the shoulders to pull her in close. She didn't want to see the hollows below the young girl's eyes fill like lakes with sorrow. "You need to get some sleep. I promise, tomorrow? Everything will get a little better. And the day after, better still. It will take a long time, and you'll stumble, but you'll get through this day even if it lasts longer than you think your heart can take."

Dolly was still, like an infant in Ethel's arms before she pulled away. Her golden hair hooked around her face and fell unkempt along her shoulders. Her eyes were steeped in fear. "I loved Ernest," she said.

"I know you did."

Dolly squeezed her hand until Ethel's countenance began to shatter. "I really, really did, Ethel."

Ethel could only nod and pull the woman back to her. She knew the agony, the anger of losing a loved one, and yet, lost in her own woe, she had forgotten that Dolly was there too, a young widow of tragic circumstance. She wasn't alone. Ethel had Dolly, and together the two women borrowed what solace they could from one another until Ethel promised, deep in her heart, that she would do all that she could for her poor, dear sister.

"We're sisters, right?" Ethel said, petting at the loose locks that fell down Dolly's back. "We'll share the load. But you should sleep now."

"I—I don't know if I can."

Ethel rose and dimmed the oil lamp whose glow lit up the room. The aureolin hue of the chambers cooled. As Dolly rose beside her, Ethel pulled back the bedclothes, and ushered the girl to lay.

"Etty?"

"Yes."

"Could you—*would* you stay?"

"Of course."

Dolly moved aside, and though Ethel was still clothed in her day clothes, she pushed off her shoes and sat down beside her, cradling Dolly's head like a mother would a sleepless child.

"You ought to write to your sisters," she suggested, looking across the room to the open door of the sitting room. "I can help you, if you want."

"No. I don't want to bother them."

Ethel glanced down, startled by her reply. "Dolly, they're your family. I can't imagine—"

"Which is why I can't..." her head was upon Ethel's lap, and her arms were wrapped around her waist like a chain.

Why? "Dolly... I—I don't understand."

"I just... I don't want to interrupt them. Their happy little lives. I don't want my woe to be theirs. I don't want their names to be a part of my tragedy. Do you understand, Ethel? Does that make... sense?"

Ethel nodded and petted the young woman's hair until the weight of Dolly's body slumped and her breathing deepened. Ethel remembered the feeling of giving up, of drowning in woe to find solace in destruction. Her family, her friends, Ethel had hated their rueful stares as she swept through life attired in grim black: a portrait of the empty grave Roland did not occupy. Their pity derived from a merriment that should have been, from their own happy threshold that she had sunk beneath with no way to grasp for the surface.

Ethel had always been floundering, until the day Dolly had gifted her a gown of pink and lace. She would make certain Dolly resurfaced. Ethel would stand on the recovering shores and hold her hand beneath the threshold *she* had never fully obtained, in order to help Dolly back and ensure she didn't fall again. And perhaps, in tandem, Ethel would also find strength of her own.

Ethel sat for a while in the dark, holding Dolly as her mind sang dirges of task and responsibility. A small clock perched on a mantelpiece nearby, chimed at eight in the evening. Slipping out from beneath her charge, Ethel tucked her sister in. She grabbed her boots and laced them, and then she left the room.

The Pavillion was a stoic place, jutting out from the corner of Great George Street. Like an ant hill, the inside consisted of corridors, plain and yet angular, that bloomed into luxurious rooms bursting with opulence and care. Ethel's room was down the hall from Dolly's, and though it was less decorated, without a sitting room, it was side by side with Beulah Murphy's, and adjoined with a mahogany door.

Ethel wasn't walking to her room, but the front parlour where she knew the lights— lit by gas—would be shimmering from the glass chandeliers. Red carpet hushed beneath her footfalls and the brushing hem of her dress, while the occasional bellhop or housekeeper wandered by.

Ethel turned to enter the front parlour, and noticed Andrew Bertram at the desk, no longer dressed in police attire. Instead, he wore a suit, the very same he adorned on the night of their first encounter, though the scent of dust was absent. His hair had been combed, and his moustache waxed, though lines of worry crept to either side of his nose and ran along the corners of his mouth.

"Miss Arsenault. Thank you for meeting with me," he said, trying to smile yet looking unsure as he did so. The room was bright yet empty. Yellow walls panelled in portraits lent the illusion of company but fell short from the empty seating that framed a hearth mottled with candles.

"I am sorry for my state of dress, Constable Bertram. I'm afraid I've yet to change." Her black wardrobe sat in a closet like the remains of a loved one and prowled in her mind like a predator.

Bertram shook his head. "Please have a seat, Miss Arsenault," he replied, gesturing to one of the many chairs in the parlour. "We have a lot to discuss."

Ethel sat and saw that a drink was already on the table between them, like a guard on patrol waiting for an impending assault. She took it and studied the contents of the glass before endeavouring a drink. She was thankful it was water and wondered if the choice of drink meant nothing worse could come from their conversation.

"I'm afraid I've grown weary of talking, Constable Bertram."

"I know. And I am sorry to bother you so soon after this morning, Miss Arsenault, but the topics I wish to discuss with you would be better off said while the pain is still fresh."

Ethel swallowed, glad for the water that kept her throat from closing. "I understand. I want—I need to know what happened, Constable."

He nodded, unbuttoning his coat as he sat opposite her on a leatherback chair. His legs were splayed as a rest for his elbows and settling his chin on the crest of folded hands, he inhaled through his nose. "This isn't going to be easy, Miss Arsenault."

She knew, and yet the challenge presented in his eyes was void of pity. For that she was grateful.

"How well did you know your brother, Miss Arsenault?"

Ethel frowned, the question more a riddle than quandary. "As well as any sister would. There were only the two of us growing up. Ernest was..." she paused to keep the memory from becoming painful, "ambitious, but also enormously kind. I daresay he grew to fit his generosity." She licked her lips to keep them moist and smiled like she had when she'd first seen him on the steps of Eden Hall.

The constable nodded behind his hands. His eyes were unfocused on the floor. "What about his relationship with his wife, Dolores?"

Dolores? Ethel made a face. The name belonged to a woman at wartime, not a bright girl standing tall in the prime of her life. "Ernest loved Dolly," Ethel said, the moniker leaving her stomach in knots. "He met her in Charlottetown, right after he moved here to invest in shipbuilding." Did Bertram suspect Dolly? Ethel frowned, the notion colouring her words. "Ernest didn't have a lot of money then, but after they wed, he bought the lot that is now Eden Hall. My father made the plans for the house and enlisted the help of a gentleman named Chappell to see it through. I met Dolly for the first time at Ernest's wedding ceremony in Summerside. She intimidated me," Ethel admitted, "if only because she was so outgoing and thrived on the social interaction of human beings."

Ethel stared at the floor and wondered how the carpet maker made the dye so closely resemble the eeking lifeblood of dying humans. "She'd be a flower wilted and pressed to die between the tabloids if the news believed she was the result of Ernest's death, Mr. Bertram." She looked into his eyes and saw they were leather, cured by seasons of crime and death, mirrors into a soul already hardened despite its youth. It disturbed her, because Ethel was certain as he gazed back into hers, Andrew Bertram saw the same.

"Miss Arsenault—"

"Ethel." She forced a smile. "Call me Ethel, please. I need not be reminded I'm the last of us, every time you address me."

Care swept into his features, and he cleared his throat as the hardness of his face softened. "In the morning, Ethel, we plan to arrest Dolly."

Her face was stone, though inside she was decaying. The assumption had been planted by the vein of his questioning, yet Ethel swallowed without the ability to accept it.

"Why?" she managed, as poised as a portrait.

He was quiet, deliberating, no doubt, on how to deliver more tragedy to a woman whose shoulders were already broken from burdens.

"There was no sign of forced entry. Ernest was shot on the second floor, with mud upon his shoes by a pistol whose ammunition matched a gun that was missing from his closet. You were poisoned. Do you think your maid could have—"

"No!" Ethel reeled from her outburst, her reddened cheeks flushed as she glanced around the quiet foyer and sat back upon the couch. "I've known Beulah my whole life. She, Ernest, and I played together as kids. She wouldn't have—"

"And yet, she came to the conclusion so quickly," he continued before Ethel could retort, holding up a hand between them. "Dolly Arsenault is our main priority at the moment. There are two officers at her door who will apprehend her in the morning. We wish for you, as a courtesy, to help deliver her with dignity into our care while we continue our investigation."

"What—" She glanced around, ensuring none of the hotel staff were within earshot. "What possible motivation could you have to suspect her?"

"I'm not really at liberty to say, Miss— Ethel."

"Constable Bertram!"

He was quiet and leant forward from his elbows. "His wealth," Andrew replied, as though ready for the question. "Ernest Arsenault was hardly home, and Dolly was often isolated. You said it yourself, Miss Arsenault, that Dolores was a socialite, and yet, it was Ernest who was favoured throughout Charlottetown."

"That's no reason—Dolly loved Ernest. Even before he was wealthy and well known."

"Perhaps," he stumbled to reply, pausing as he shifted upon his chair. His voice was faint in an effort to sound soft. "Miss— Ethel." He sighed, massaging at his palms. "We have reasonable doubt to believe there was a burglar, and yet Dolly was the first to implicate an unknown assailant. If she's lying, then she has something to hide, and if there was no intruder, then someone in the house killed Ernest."

Ethel stared until her eyes watered and welled with tears. She didn't wish to look away. It would imply the logic in Bertram's presumption held weight, and yet... what could Ethel say when doubt was rending her asunder?

"We don't intend to take her until morning."

"Where will you take her?"

"To Falconwood for a time, then..." he didn't have to finish. If Dolly were arrested and convicted of murder, she'd go to jail, then prison, then God only knows...

As it was, Falconwood was a lunatic asylum, nestled far from the core of Charlottetown near Hillsborough. It had once housed victims of contagious disease. Why they'd put Dolly there was uncanny, though Ethel was certain that Constable Bertram thought it a service.

"How long will she have to stay there?" she asked, biting her lip.

"Until she confesses, or we find the culprit."

She noted the delivery of the response and how the inflection of his voice indicated how less likely the latter possibility was.

"Will there be a trial?"

"Of course, but I'm afraid until we have gathered enough evidence, she will have to reside in Falconwood. It's safer there, for a woman, and without the hope of bail, she may have to stay several months."

There would be no bail, not if Dolly was a suspect in Ernie's murder. All his assets would be frozen to her. It didn't seem fair, in great part because Ethel couldn't believe

Dolly would do such a thing. Yet, who else in the house could have?

"What if it was..." Ethel stopped short as her visions of ghosts, phantoms, and creatures spawned cruel and unlikely alternatives. Which was more probable? A spectre in the dark, or a wife who'd lied and killed her husband?

Ethel shook her head and swallowed down her doubts as she gripped her hands to keep them from shaking.

"Early morning. Come quietly," she whispered. "Allow her to dress. Have a stagecoach ready. The blinds should be drawn."

"Absolutely," Bertram replied, matching his volume to hers. "Until this is resolved, we all must sustain our propriety." She watched him stand and button his coat, and the gentle scent of dust snaked into her nostrils.

"Mr. Bertram?" Ethel asked, watching as his stone mask fell back across his face.

"Yes, Miss Ethel?"

She couldn't help but note his eyes, which glimmered with concern from behind an iron curtain. "Be careful of my family, please."

He walked away, and Ethel stayed, until all she felt was empty.

Chapter 10

It was a bright morning, the kind that could inspire even the poorest of souls. The sun came up and smiled on all that clung to its auroral skirts while Ethel watched its daytime blanket fall upon Charlottetown from the window of her bedroom.

She hadn't slept but sat upon her bed and wondered at the sunrise that promised life, love, and hope on a day she wished would never arrive. Perhaps the sun—that hung alone in the darkest part of Heaven—was lending succour because it knew how lonely the darkness was. The brightest thing in all the world, also knew the depths of the abyss, because within its pit it dwelt and shone its rays outward in hope to lend comfort to those beyond.

Ethel had wanted to sprint like a mad fox back towards Dolly's room the moment Bertram had left. Instead, she remained in the hotel's parlour and watched as a heavy set man, spangled with polished buttons and his officers badge, walked towards her sister's room. Outside he stood, like an unknown guardian to the rest of the Pavillion's patrons. Protecting Charlottetown from sweet Dolly Arsenault.

Of course, Ethel knew that he was there to keep them separated until daybreak forced the path onward, but the thought that Dolly should awaken alone was agonising, if only because Ethel had promised to stay.

Her room was cold, and her breath made ghosts in the air as she wandered to wash and dress. Beulah lay sleeping in the adjoining room, exhaustion a heavy crown upon the young maid's brow. Ethel had heard her cry several times during the night, moaning, tossing in an effort to thwart the demons that were heralding the sunrise. Ethel didn't wake Beulah, for Dolly's sake and the sake of the rest that they would all sorely need in the coming days.

The Pavillion, now less a pleasant lodge of hospitality and more a stable of unnerving inevitabilities, was quiet. The silence hung like Damocles' sword as Ethel marched towards Dolly's room. Daylight warmed the panelled windows of the hotel's halls, and maids already bustled through the winding corridors, but in Ethel's mind, all was still. Though the gas-lit lights were off, the outside world was mirrored back at her as Ethel watched her reflection in its glass.

In black, she looked like the grim reaper, whose presence was fit enough to usher in a person's ill-fated future. That her presence was to be a comfort for Mrs. Arsenault, seemed ironic. What words could she say to ease the plight of her sister? What words did Ethel have but the hollow and pitiful pleas that everything would be all right? Words she did not believe in herself.

She didn't say anything when she arrived at Dolly's door. The officer moved like the great beast Cerberus, sliding to the side to let one more soul into the Hadean heart of the opulent bedchamber. Though outside was a portrait of pleasant weather and airy light, inside Dolly's room, Ethel had to light a lamp. It shone like a wisp amongst treasure troves. Heavy curtains that blocked the day were drawn, and sleeping in the centre, like a doll whose companion absconded, was what Constable Bertram believed to be the beast that killed her brother.

Lovely, bright, happy Ernest, who lived now as a memory that would fade over time. His wife was asleep, her breast rising and falling like the keel of a boat upturned at sea. Ethel was glad that her entrance had not awoken the girl nor did her trek across the room stir the young woman from rest.

She laid the lamp upon a dressing bureau, and then searched through hastily prepared trunks for a suitable dress. Nothing of Dolly's was suitable. It was all patterned and jovial, with lace and flowers and light colours. If she thought Dolly would fit them, Ethel would have gifted her one of her own gowns. Mourning clothes Ethel had aplenty, and they may have garnered sympathy from any early morning onlookers that chanced to see Dolly being shuffled inside a stagecoach.

Ethel loathed to see her in black however, especially adorned in a gown *she* had brought from Summerside.

"Etty?"

Ethel turned, grief clawing at her features. Dolly was sitting up, her long hair less flouncy than usual. It stuck to either side of her face and pulled at her features until her cheeks seemed to hang above the corners of her downturned lips. Spectres of light that insisted past the heavy curtains, sent shadows over the bed.

Ethel bent towards the trunk and hefted a gown of white lace to lay at the foot of the bed. It was simplistic compared to the other gowns Dolly owned, but Ethel hoped the image of white would lend credence to her sister's innocence.

"I'm sorry to wake you, Dolly," Ethel replied as she moved to sit beside the bed. There were hairpins on the nightstand and a brush made from ivory. "Let me do your hair?" she asked, smiling as the woman shuffled across the mattress to sit beside her.

"It seems so early. Did morning even come?"

"It did. However, we're not yet ready to face it. Let us get you dressed."

Dolly's hair was snarled, and her skin smelled of salt and brine like she had been sleeping in the sea. "I'm sorry Etty, that you have to wear black again. I... I—"

"Shh. Everything is going to be all right. Let us put you together. You'll feel better then, and it will be easier to confront the day, confront all… the unpleasantness.”

By noon Dolly would be sitting in a cell somewhere, while Ethel contemplated whether her sister-in-law could have killed her brother.

“Are you hungry?”

“No.”

Ethel pursed her lips, pinning another lock in place as she glanced at a bottle of spirits winking in the corner. Doubts of Dolly’s compassion were waving banners in her head, but Ethel shook them down. There was no feasible way that Ernest’s wife, whom he loved more than anything, could have killed him. There had to be something more, something sinister…

“Listen Dolly, I need to tell you something,” Ethel said when they had finally dressed and prepared her for the day. Ethel sat on the bed beside her but jumped to fetch a glass of spirits. “Drink this first, it should help.” She didn’t know if it would, only that she had seen her father take a dram to calm his nerves when the news was sour.

“Etty, what is going on?” Dolly asked, taking a pull of the proffered drink.

The silence between them was telling. Ethel tried in vain to pluck the gentlest words to describe what was about to happen, but she saw panic strike the young woman’s features.

“Etty, you’re scaring me.”

"Listen, Dolly," she said again, like a mother who promised to fix it all. "There are constables outside. They are going to take you to Falconwood. They believe you killed my brother." Why Ethel hadn't described him in relation to their nuptial connections, she wasn't sure, but the clumsiness of it tied her tongue in knots as Dolly's panic threatened to pour past her throat in something visceral.

"It's going to be all right," Ethel said, tucking Dolly in towards the hollow at her throat. "You must not yell or make a scene. You must go with the constables and hold yourself up confidently." *But not so much that they think you callous.* "I will get everything in order while you're gone."

"Ethel," she cried, forcing herself away, "You don't think I did such a thing, do you?"

Dolly's face was a litany of woe, and for all the world, as Ethel looked into the young girl's face, she thought she'd never forgive herself for considering such a creature could harm her brother.

"No," Ethel said at once, pulling Dolly back into her shoulder. She was unable to keep the well of tears from spilling on her cheeks. "But you need to listen and do as the officers say. We will get to the bottom of this. We will find who did such a thing."

"Why is this happening?"

Ethel's resolve was breaking, the fissures of her heart worming into the countenance of the now widow that sobbed within her arms. She was clutching at Dolly's back now, to keep herself from shaking, and though it felt like seconds had passed, it must have been more because the door spilled open.

Constable Bertram, looking stern and melancholy like a sinking ship, walked inside the room. Abreast was another man, older but less sure.

"Mrs. Arsenault, you have to come with us."

Dolly sat up, a few discordant curls falling out of place as she spun on her heel. "This is a mistake! All of it. I never killed Ernie, I would *never*—"

"Mrs. Arsenault, the police have granted you liberties that were beyond our obligations. I would advise you to come with dignity." His eyes caught Ethel's, and his glance was of earnest request.

She leapt from the bed like a shadow late to follow. "Listen to the constable, Dolly. Was he not your friend?" Ethel embraced her sister's shoulders, proffering strength and balance as Dolly stood up straighter.

"I'm scared, Etty."

Ethel quaked, her words boulders in her mouth. "They'll keep you safe. They'll find who did it and put them away."

"What if they don't?" She backed away. The police moved up to escort her. "What if they never find out who did it?"

"Don't worry, Mrs. Arsenault. Your husband was a well-respected man in Charlottetown. We *will* find the culprit."

"Will you, Constable Bertram?" Ethel whispered from the room as the door yawned wide at their departure. *What if the murderer was* not *Dolly. And what if the murderer* struck *again?*

Chapter 11

Ethel looked down at the sea of mud kicked up from the rain that had swept the southern coasts of Charlottetown. Along the planks that sunk into the slurping void of the city roads, people huddled in their coats as they went about their day-to-day, hemlines rust red and dripping with filth. Even the buildings thronged together on the banks of Great George Street seemed to slump, like tombstones falling into the very graves they were meant to commemorate. Beside her, Beulah was quiet, watching as Ethel glanced at a stagecoach struggling through the muck.

On days like these, most people had to walk, but as the two ladies waited at the corner of the Pavillion, they heard the squelch of the approaching mud wagon that was meant to ferry them back to Eden Hall.

Old and splintered, the wagon lumbered forwards like an aged creature attempting to hoist its body out of the sopping ground. Less than a stone's throw away, another coach was marooned with its whole front left wheel in the mud. Several young men groaned as they struggled to pull it up, while a young mother, beneath a store-top awning, tried to soothe her squalling baby.

It had been several days, and though the noises in the city's core were typical on a sunny day, Ethel was much relieved to be leaving the confines of the grand hotel. Since Dolly was removed and carted away to Falconwood, Ethel had been in perpetual limbo. She was unsure what had to be done or whether she wished to do anything but grieve for herself, her family, and her sister.

But she had promised to help, and Eden Hall was empty now. Affairs must be set in order. Ernest deserved to be put to rest with dignity, and while his wife was in Falconwood, it fell to Ethel to pick up the pieces.

She hadn't wanted to return to Eden Hall, whose name itself was a ragged mockery. If she had obeyed her impulse, Ethel would have left for Summerside as soon as Dolly's wagon had vanished behind the looming properties. But she couldn't, not without unyielding shame and with no other place to go, Ethel found herself again enroute to her brother's mansion, made glum and chilling by his absence.

"I'll prepare you something warm, Miss Ethel," Beulah insisted as they climbed the stairs to the outside porch. The stained glass windows winked with beaded raindrops, but as the mahogany door was hauled open, the scent of must joined the damp outside like two tides colliding.

"I suppose I'll have to start a fire first." Beulah made a noise as she shrugged off her coat and rubbed the warmth back into her arms. There was a shawl on a chair by the entryway, and she grabbed it after hanging her jacket and then helping Ethel out of hers. "Put this on." Beulah handed the wrap to Ethel. "You don't want to catch a cold. Perhaps it would be best if you rested while I got the house heated."

Ethel had been staring at the staircase, wondering if at the top the burglar had been waiting for her brother. Did the assailant rush him first? Or was the gun nozzle the first and last thing Ernest saw.

"I don't want to go upstairs," she said. What if she saw a remnant of that night? Some little thing left behind like a bloodstain or a nick in the wood. What if the body was still beneath the white, linen blanket? Saying so would concern Miss Murphy, so Ethel cleared her throat. "It seems the police have left behind a mess. It will warm me up to help you clean, so please," she smiled, pinching at the shawl to draw it closer, "allow me to do it."

Beulah nodded and with a sigh, turned to lament the state of the house. Everything seemed out of place. The rugs were askew, glasses and dishware left out, while muddied footprints stamped across the floor and dust crept over the furnishings. It was easier to focus on the tasks at hand, and though Beulah huffed at the disorder the police left behind, Ethel thought it a mercy that they had given them something to keep their minds from wandering.

They started in the kitchen first, stoking the fires, and washing the dishes while preparing dinner for later. Beulah had found a half-filled box of limes under the counter and promised she'd make key lime pie, a dessert she came across in an old recipe book years ago.

After the kitchen, they moved to the downstairs den and then into the dining room. Ethel knew eventually she'd have to venture into Ernest's study, but instructed Beulah to leave it for now until she was ready to search for Ernest's will and legal papers.

"You ought to ask Constable Bertram for help," Beulah suggested with her arm across Ethel's shoulders. Ernest's study was dark. The liquor bottles and emptied glasses winked from atop his large oak desk and mantlepiece. His gun cabinet, inherited from their father years ago, was on the far wall. Next to it, a window that could be opened in the summer to allow one to step into the side yard garden, was shuttered. Everywhere were papers.

"Constable Bertram... I suppose I should ask him for help." Bertram had told her that a gun from the cabinet was missing, and the bullets removed from Ernest's body were similar to those used in the missing firearm. Ethel didn't know anything about weapons, but she was aware that the gun cabinet had been a topic of pride for their father. Rooted even in their family name and history, those were stories her father had told Ernest. Tales of war, heroism, and galloping soldiers. Perhaps if Ernest and Dolly had ever birthed a son or daughter, Ernie would have passed those stories down. Now they were shades of the past, locked inside a cabinet with a missing gun.

But why would a gun go missing? Ethel furrowed her brow, hearing the grandfather clock upstairs chime out the dinnertime hour. Ernest's pride in their father's gun collection was hardy. He never would have lost a firearm. *Didn't he keep the cabinet locked, like their father always had?*

"Let's go, Miss Ethel. The meat pie ought to be ready by now, and I am aching to try that lime dessert."

Tomorrow, Ethel thought, wandering away from Ernest's den to the kitchen. She'd contemplate that all tomorrow. For now, she had to conquer the stairs and the landing where Ernest died. But even then, she'd do *that* after supper.

A knock on the front door was followed by an awkward cough and holler. Both Ethel and Beulah looked up from the kitchen countertop, having just set the plates for their evening meal, ears straining to hear the greeting from the backside of the house. As the women approached, all that followed were several more loud knocks and the pattering of wet feet shuffling on the patio.

Ethel called out, glancing through the stained glass that framed either side of the large front door. Whoever it was, doddered back and forth, running their hands through their hair as they turned to glance towards the road. Their boots were heavy and thumped like the carcass of a doe upon a game cart. Ethel's hand paused, her fingers poised to grip the brass knob handle. What if this person, this guest, was dangerous? Was she opening Eden Hall to friends or serpents?

She pursed her lips, a whistle of wind from beneath the door heralding her to hurry and respond.

"Goddamn it, weren't they coming home today? I swore she said today. Where the Hell's that pap—"

"Mr. Carlow?"

"Aloysius?"

Al Carlow leapt, almost skidding over the wet floorboards of the outside porch. His short, cropped hair was wet but slicked back. A few rogue strands stuck to the slope of his brow as he committed himself to not falling prone. His shirt, suspenders, and trousers were dry from the calf up.

"Jesus H. Christ!" he yelled, rushing to excuse himself. "I-I'm sorry, Miss Arsenault. I didn't mean—"

"Would you call me Ethel? *Miss* Ethel, if you'd prefer."

Al was already nodding.

"It's just, hearing that name right now, in this big empty house is... isolating." She was holding the door and looking towards the harbour that crowned the crest of the field before it. Pinning a smile in place like a butterfly, Ethel let the door yawn wider.

"Won't you come in, Mr. Carlow? We were just sitting down to eat if you'd like to join us. Beulah?" Ethel looked back, her eyes settling on the wide-open gaze of her maidservant.

"Ye-yes, Miss Ethel?" she replied, brushing at her skirts to manage her shaking hands.

"Is it... all right?" Ethel kept space in the doorway as Al Carlow stood in the rain outside. He was as still as a moored coach in the mud but, as Beulah nodded and walked forward to take Ethel's place, his boots thudded across the threshold.

"Of course. Come on in," Beulah said, closing the door behind him before turning on her heel to leave. "I'll set out another plate. There's enough for an army, though you're only allowed one slice of lime pie." The slight shake of her voice gave her away. Beulah's poorly manufactured ire whispered of something more as she hastened to depart Al's presence.

"Thank you, Miss Ethel. I'm so sorry I didn't meet with you earlier. Ernest was a good man, a *great* man to work for. I—" he stammered, blinking in an effort to keep himself whole. "I'm so terribly sorry this all happened."

"As am I, Mr. Carlow," Ethel didn't have the energy to put on a brave face, and in the midst of friends, she thought that was all right. What was to happen to Al and Adella and all the serving lads and lasses now that Ernie was gone? Ethel would figure that out later. Right now, she wanted a hot meal, something in her belly to keep her sturdy when she ventured up the stairs.

"Let me get you something warm to drink. Come, we've set up in the kitchen."

Sitting in the dining room seemed wrong somehow. Without Dolly or Ernest, Ethel thought she'd feel dwarfed by the empty chairs and stark placement of dinnerware. In the kitchen, where the stove and the heat were welcoming, all three of them sat around a countertop, the very same Dolly had been slicing limes at the first night Ethel caught her downstairs. Copper and cast-iron pots cluttered the walls, while dried herbs, glassware, and preservatives collected on shelves around the room. Adjacent to the wood stove, was the door to the basement. The laundry and the larder were beyond, secured behind the iron latch of the door handle. A small pantry was opposite the kitchen's main entrance, just to the right of the servants' corridors.

It was a crowded room, workable, but with every available space filled with purpose and design. As the three of them sat, soaking in the scent of bread baking, Ethel sighed. Their meal was good, the meat pie hearty and filling. Hot tea and coffee accompanied their dinner and was a suitable retreat when words refused to flow. For the most part, all three were quiet, the woe of the last few days pushed aside as they nourished their bodies for the hard conversations ahead. It was a comfort at least, to dine together, even though Ethel was certain the air between Miss Murphy and Al Carlow was tainted by something more.

When they had begun to clear away the plates, Mr. Carlow lingered at the door, leaning on its frame as he jangled keys in his trouser pocket. He was chewing on his cheek, making a subtle glance at Miss Murphy now and again when he thought no one was looking. After a while, however, perhaps in an effort to alleviate the awkward silence, he stood up straight and rubbed his lips together.

"I need to tell ya, Miss Ethel, that the day all this," he waved his hands between them as though searching for the right word, "*unpleasantness* happened, Fritz took a heart attack. He's all right," he continued before Ethel could shout out, "I brought him to my sister's so she could look after him awhile... but I think all this—I think it was all too much for him."

Ethel glanced at Miss Murphy and took a seat on an old wooden stool next to one of the countertops. Her heart was beating in her chest, and a barrage of happy memories flashed like a falling deck of cars in her periphery.

"He's all right?" she echoed, taking the slight nod from Aloysius as an antidote to her budding fear. She took a deep breath in. "I need to visit him."

"We can go tomorrow," Beulah agreed. "We can bring some fresh bread."

"My sister lives on Dorchester, a few roads up from Water Street. Her husband works on the ships, but he's been home the last few weeks. If ya have a scrap of paper and something to write with, I can scribble her address."

Ethel nodded, swallowing to keep her mouth from going dry. Al excused himself after that, saying he had work in the stables and mud to wash off. Though Ethel wanted to head straight up to bed, instead, she stayed down to help Beulah with the dishes. It seemed like every single cup and saucer was dirty, but the menial tasks were greater than her desire to sit alone with only a wall as a barricade to her brother's final moments.

What if I go up there and...
What? What could happen?

The stairs were prelude, like a spade at work in the boneyard. As they attained the second floor, Ethel and Beulah saw that the hall was pristine. The floorboards, once disguised with white linen covers, were unstained, while the walls had been wiped down, and no remnant of chalk was evident upon the floor. As Ethel let her breathing settle, she clasped Beulah by the hand as they marched towards her bedroom door.

Everything was normal. There was no marker that spoke of Ernest's death. Nothing.

"I don't want to linger too long. I want to see Fritz after breakfast," Ethel said, running her hands down the grainy surface of the oakwood door. As soon as they'd entered her room, she'd shut it closed, and now, leaning upon it, the frame pressed grooves into her fingertips.

"I understand, Miss Ethel, and I'm sorry I—about myself and Mr. Carlow."

Ethel's eyes floated from the polished floorboards towards her servant's gaze. Beulah Murphy was her oldest and fondest friend, around even when Ethel had been a seedling sprouting at her mother's stalk.

I still have you, don't I, Beulah?

Ethel smiled, though the corners of her eyes slanted downward. Letting go of the threshold, she reached between them and cupped Beulah's cheek. In the belly of the grandfather clock down the hall, the hour struck almost on cue.

Beulah winced.

"If we both weren't hurting so much, I'd tease you for your happiness." *Even while I'm jealous of it.* Ethel's eyes didn't catch Beulah's as she looked away, but neither did Ethel wait for their return. "I'm glad you have it," Ethel continued. "Happiness. Even small bits of it. Keep it as something to cling to." She pressed her fists into her chest and was dazed as the floor rose to secure her eye. Her parents were gone, Roland, Ernest... Dolly...

But here was Beulah, who'd also suffered, apologising for an instant of happiness that dared to share the hour that her brother died.

"If you don't mind, I may cling to your happiness too, Beulah... if only by our close bond and proximity."

Chapter 12

The door clicked closed and, like some beast of the night ready to bury themselves in slumber, Ethel eyed the four poster bed with feral thirst. She wanted to lay amidst the sheets and pretend that she was numb, fossilising into oil that shared in the remains of her family. Instead, she grabbed her Gladstone, sat upon the bed, and rummaged through her letters and papers until she found her journal. Bits of charcoal were tucked in a pocket in the lining of the bag, and she extracted them, tossing back the cover of the book to the unmarked sheets at the end.

She needed to draw him, sketch out her brother's face to his exact likeness. Her fingers were shaking, the dried blood long leftover from the previous page stained the sketch from behind.

Why is it so hard? Why is the charcoal not smearing as I intend? Why is his jaw too thin, too fat, too irregular? The coal was unfamiliar, frustrating her attempts. Ethel rubbed it on the page in black clouds until it was smoke upon her fingers.

Why can't I draw him?

Because all she could see was the white linen on the floor.

Roland had had no body, and despite her woe, there was blind hope that the well of despair she had succumbed to would fill and rise to the ledge. Instead, it had drowned her, eventually, but it was an eventuality she saw coming.

Ernest's death was less a disease and more a limb rent from one's body. It was so fast, she'd forgotten to see him, to remember what he looked like the instant before he'd been there.

Ethel wept, and the coal upon her fingers fouled her cheeks and palms. She wished she had a photograph. Just one to place within her book and cover the stain from the previous page.

"Dolly..." Ethel glanced up, a lantern beyond the bedclothes curtain glimmering through the fabric like nixies and sprites. *Dolly may have a picture.* Ethel was certain that she did. When Ernest had returned to Summerside to plan out Eden Hall, he had a picture with him. A memento of the dear couple standing in front of a magnolia tree in blossom.

She had forgotten about it. Her father had been amazed, not only by the loveliness of Ernie's to-be-wife but by the means by which he possessed her inside his pocket, on a square of black and white paper.

Surely Dolly had another?

Ethel walked across the bedroom, slipping out the door and wiping the soot upon her sleeves. The halls were already cold, like a garden in winter. Across the landing, opposite the grandfather clock, was another set of stairs that led up towards the master's chamber. Ethel had never been inside the actual room, though she recalled from her father's blueprints that it was large and across an open hall that looked out towards the bay. Essentially, their room was above her own on the top floor of the Queen Anne's turret.

Ethel took a small lamp from a table in the hall and lit it. She was careful that her footfalls didn't cause unwanted groans as she climbed the small set of winding stairs to the third floor. Pictures with gold trim lined the dark green walls of the upper floor, while light from the outside laid across the hall in carpets.

Ethel knew that somewhere, beyond the dim, panelled, emerald walls, there was a hidden stairwell down towards the kitchens. It was small and slight, a mouse-like labyrinth made for the many intended maids that had been planned in the Hall's design.

A chaise lounge lay before the three cathedral windows that watched the bay. Ethel imagined Dolly lying down upon it, a throw to keep her legs warm as she wrote in her diary or read aloud a poem she had been fond of.

The door to the master bedroom was a solid oak and was closed as Ethel approached. A knob of brass with whirling designs caught the light of her lamp and sparkled in the darkness. It was warm when she grasped it and gave way easily as she leant forward to enter.

As a boy, Ernie's room had been sparse. The few adornments their mother had used to decorate were admired by the maids when it was time for dusting. This room, however, was resplendent. There was a portrait of Dolly that her brother was happy to enclose himself in.

The walls were high and rounded into a crowned ceiling that draped with heavy curtains. They framed the windows that looked out towards the water and were cinched about the middle like a lady's waist with gold tassel ropes. The green from the hall spilled into the bedchamber, though the walls inside were capped with a decorative ribbon of burnished gold paisley. The bedclothes upon the grand, four poster bed, mimicked the Persian style of the rugs upon the floor, while a fireplace yawned opposite the bed and was abreast of a polished baroque vanity whose mirror climbed the wall.

If Dolly had been a royal sequestered away in a tower by a dragon, Ethel was certain it would be in a room like this, where anyone would have been content. The worth of Eden Hall was contained within this room, and staring at it, Ethel's eyes watered at its majestic wonder. It was surreal, and yet as her pause lingered, Ethel shook her head, feeling like a child sitting uninvited in the sweet shop.

She had to find a picture. *Take it and leave, and let the room dwell alone until its Mistress returns.*

Ethel walked to the vanity, glancing over the winking bottles of perfume and tins of cosmetics. Guttered candles spilled over their brass holders, while a book of pressed flowers lay open upon the tabletop. An ivory case sprawled with pearls, chains, and delicate charms, while an open drawer of bangles and ornate hairpins glittered from within the velvet-lined box.

Ethel rummaged through the shining chattels, glancing in the drawers and boxes filled with treasures. Much of Dolly's gemstones had been left behind, abandoned in the wake of Ernest's death and their hasty departure to the Pavillion hotel. Ethel thought perhaps there would be a locket, or a memento with his picture, but her search was in vain.

Maybe Dolly brought it with her to the hotel... If she had, then the trunks were still at the hotel, waiting to be delivered.

Ethel sat upon the vanity's chair and looked through the window towards the front lawn of Eden Hall. It was dark but for a single streetlight that flickered behind rain-spotted glass.

She wondered at the hoard of treasures and the room and its grandeur. A room like this was ordinary in a house as stately as Eden Hall. Was it these trinkets that the burglar had sought? Was Ernest's life worth a trove of costly gems?

No. But then Ethel had never gone hungry.

She recalled the silver swallows. A gift she'd meant for the couple on the morning of Ernest's departure. She had them still, tucked away in a forgotten box beneath her bed like a casket of hope and prosperity.

It brought to mind a brooch, and standing again to look through the vanity, Ethel stood agape at its absence. It had been silver and garnet and tucked into Dolly's collar on the day of Ethel's arrival to the hall. That Beulah had seen a similar one at a shop was curious, but now that it was missing from the vanity, Ethel wondered at its meaning

Had the burglar come again? No. They wouldn't have left so much behind. Perhaps it was misplaced? Ethel would have been content with the idea if she hadn't found an empty case in the lowest drawer of the golden vanity.

Maybe there are simply two... and Dolly has the other.

Ethel rubbed at her temples, the thrumming of her heartbeat resounding in her head like thundering drums. She was building mysteries like walls around her

140

woe, and the night was happy to oblige the mood.

She tucked the gems back into place, closed the drawers, and hurried out the room. Tears were falling over her cheeks, and they stung her eyes like fresh wounds.

I need to sleep. I need to... stop thinking about everything and just... disappear for a while.

The door fell closed like a mausoleum. The halls beyond gaped. Even the stairs to the second floor, once silent and still, moaned as she descended.

Sleep. Just go to sleep, Ethel. It will all make sense in the morning.

It wouldn't, but despite herself, she shook her head and rushed to her room from the landing. Outside was cold, the halls were smothering, and as Ethel climbed into bed and beneath the covers, she couldn't shake the eyes she felt upon her.

Chapter 13

Whether it was thunder or the snap of a lion's roar, the day began with rain as its prologue. Ethel stirred around four in the morning, her head a dome of eerie thoughts. Dreams of burglars that hid in the shadows gave way to restlessness, and so creeping downstairs, Ethel sought paradise in labour. She examined the pantry, put on the kettle, and stoked the fires. She hoped to start breakfast before Beulah awoke. To surprise her friend in bed with breakfast, might become the preamble to brighter days, a step away from the melancholy that drew its pall over Eden Hall. Ethel knew it was, even if she knew it wasn't.

Beulah came downstairs after an hour and helped finish the breakfast. They both had to go through papers today. "Wills, bills, and whatnot," Ethel mumbled as she hefted up a sack of flour. "But I think we should go pay a visit to Fritz before all that. Let's be sure to make extra bread to gift." She was kneading the set dough from the night before. A streak of flour blazed across her forehead.

Beulah nodded. "The poor man... and let's make some for Mrs. Kennedy as well, for allowing him to stay."

By mid-afternoon, they had adorned their coats and buttoned their gloves in preparation for their soggy promenade. The constant clap of thunder followed by the applause of rain had halted to an ornery grey for their departure. Though the roads were mires, the wagon would be stout enough to ferry them down to Dorchester.

Ethel tucked a basket of bread beneath her arm and looked over to Beulah. "Have you got the umbrellas?" she asked, nodding thanks as Beulah approached to hand her one. They stood on the inside of the door to wait for the wagon.

As if on cue, a set of footfalls thumped across the hollow porch, and Ethel moved to open the door. She came up short and almost blundered into Constable Bertram before bounding back across the threshold.

"Mr. Bertram!" Ethel gasped, clutching at her chest. Bertram was stoic, as unmoving as the columns framing the verandah, though he must have been just as surprised as she. "I thought you were Al with the wagon," she explained, taking in a deep breath to calm her nerves.

Constable Bertram looked wet, like he had been walking in the rain all his life. His hair beneath the rim of his hat was sodden and dripping with water, while the long hem of his coat was soaked up to his waist.

"Do you want to come in? Get dry?"

He shook his head and doffed his hat, looking between both women as though only expecting the one. "I'm sorry to bother you, Miss Ethel. I was hoping to get here earlier, but my coach got stuck in the mud. Are you unavailable at the moment?"

Ethel stepped back to allow the constable to stand inside the dry foyer. "We were just about to leave, actually. An old friend of ours, Fritz Humphry, had a heart attack a few nights ago."

Bertram's shock split across his stolid features and he looked away, as though puzzling with a jigsaw. "Is he all right? What happened?"

Ethel smiled, though it was more a frown made light. "We think perhaps the shock of—" She looked away. "The shock of it all was too much for him."

"I'm sorry."

"It's all right. I'm relieved to say he's reported as fine now. We were, in fact, about to leave to bring him and his keeper some bread."

Bertram's chest deflated, as though set free from any worry. "I was hoping perhaps to speak to you a bit. Would it be all right if I asked to share your wagon?"

"I think Miss Ethel deserves a wee break from the pol—"

"No, Beulah, it's all right. He's trying to help Dolly, remember?" At least, Ethel hoped that was his aim. If nothing else, finding Ernie's killer and bringing him to justice was paramount, *right?* "I'd be glad to share," she continued, following his stare as it flitted towards Beulah.

Ethel frowned, her back teeth grinding. *Why would Constable Bertram trust me, and not trust Beulah?* No doubt when discussing the case, he didn't wish a potential suspect to be present. But Beulah was innocent. *A police's mistrust is a part of his job…* Ethel determined she'd have to help him come to the same conclusion.

"Beulah," Ethel called, turning on her heel. She took her by the hands and squeezed, hoping that the gesture said enough. "I need you to stay here. I need you to prepare the den for later. Constable Bertram will escort me to Mrs. Kennedy's."

Beulah looked agape but nodded. A knowing stare was exchanged between both women before Miss Murphy strode forward to press another basket beneath the constable's arm. "Don't let the bread get wet," she grumbled to him, looking back with concern in her eyes. "Are you certain, Miss Ethel?"

"I'll be safe. I'm sorry to leave you."

Beulah laughed, a hopeful woe beading in her eyes. "Well, I suppose some time to myself would be good. If you cry in the dark all the time, you'll get wrinkles," she said as she unbuttoned her jacket.

Ethel sniffed, but mirrored her mirth, stepping in to offer the woman a fond farewell.

"Have her back before supper please, Constable."

"I'll only be as long as Miss Ethel permits," he replied, donning his hat with a nod as he moved to descend the porch stairs.

Ethel watched him go. *What had he arrived for?*

Thanking Miss Murphy, she returned to the porch and walked until the constable let her pass. Ethel saw the mud wagon down the road, lobbing clumps of dirt in its wake. A few men were out with their horses, and the poor beasts were caked right up to their bellies. She imagined the introduction of automobiles to Charlottetown, great metal caskets moored in the mud. *Sure, you'd stay dry, but you'd never get anywhere.*

With Constable Bertram's help, Ethel climbed the small stair to enter the wagon. It creaked from side to side as both passengers arranged themselves. There were windows on either side of the coach, with wood slats that had been installed to keep the mud from splashing into the cab. They were open only enough to let in a bit of light.

"I... know these last few days have been hard, Miss Arsenault." Bertram began after a considering pause, "and I know that Dolly's arrest has... only compounded the situation for you—"

"It seems you know everything, Constable Bertram. Have you come with good news? Are you to now relay the culprit behind my brother's murder?" The snap of her voice was accompanied by instant regret as she sighed and looked towards the floor.

"I'm sorry, Miss—"

Ethel held up her hand. "No. *I'm* sorry, Constable Bertram. You're right, it has been a hard few days. But despite your inclination towards my sister-in-law's guilt, I know you are trying your best on my family's behalf. I *am* truly grateful."

Constable Bertram cleared his throat and rummaged in his coat for a pipe. Outside, they passed another coach mired in the mud and a few jolly kids who seemed fond of making a mess of their attire.

"I wanted to tell you that your sister-in-law, Mrs. Arsenault, is being treated well at Falconwood, and if you wish to visit her, arrangements can be made."

Ethel glanced across and caught his eyes. The cold of the rain had stained his cheeks with a flush of crimson, and the cut of his jaw carried the colour to his ears. He puffed upon his pipe as they rode along, his moustache settling above his lip in a manner resembling earnestness, but as his eyes flitted from her face to the window, Ethel caught a whisper of boyish unease.

She was touched. It was like a chain had gone slack around the barrel of her chest. Ethel determined she would go and see Dolly as soon as she was able. Falconwood was situated on the northeast coast of the Hillsborough River, and with the roads in such a state, Ethel was certain that Aloysius would beg her to wait a few more days. But it was something to look forward to, at least, that was what she hoped.

"Thank you, Constable. I appreciate that." A spark of emotion plumed in her belly but was short-lived.

"You say you're going to visit your friend?"

Ethel cleared her throat and ran her hands down the braided band of the breadbasket on her lap. The other sat beside Bertram on the stagecoach bench. "Mr. Fritz Humphry," she agreed with a nod of her head. Ethel slid her teeth along her bottom lip and sighed. "He's worked with my family for years. He was a labourer of my father's back in the day. He doesn't say much, but Mr. Humphrey's been around since I was a girl, and we are all very fond of him."

"He joined you on your journey here from Greens Shore, Summerside?"

Ethel inclined her head. "Ernest sent Mr. Carlow to collect us all. In the slight case that the journey proved cumbersome, Mr. Humphrey wanted to accompany Beulah and I. He resolved he'd take the trek back to Summerside alone when we had settled."

"And the shock of your brother's death caused—"

"The heart attack, yes." They were focused now, the slight distractions outside the coach muted by the conversation. The tone in his voice was an orchestra, and Ethel couldn't help but hear a low base of suspicion.

"Who *found* Mr. Humphrey, Miss Ethel?" He looked out the window, watching as streets went by as though bored of the topic. Ethel wondered if Mr. Bertram thought all women were that dull.

"Aloysius found him."

"Is that what he said?"

Ethel pursed her lip, befuddled by the questions. "Why, yes. But I don't understand your train of thought, Constable. Do you mean to insinuate that Mr. Carlow is somehow suspect?"

Andrew frowned, chewing at his cheek as he let the pause linger.

Ethel held his gaze.

"He's *certainly* suspect. Al Carlow is a man who is under the employ of your brother. He is unceremoniously courting your serving woman, who is a close friend of the family, and mayhap your brother forbade it?" He tossed his head, as though evaluating the likelihood of the theory. "Or maybe, Ernest didn't even know. But let's theorise that Ernest Arsenault came in, thought there was a burglar, attacked, and was shot dead because Al was sneaking into your maid's chambers." He stopped and caught her eyes, waiting to see if the levity of his theory was too much for her to bear. There was a hint of concern in the quake of his brow, but as Ethel froze, waiting for her body to respond, her mind knew that if even a hint of woe shone through, the constable would bar her from his investigation. It couldn't be *too much for her*.

She closed her eyes and opened her mouth, inhaling deeply before replying, "So you think Mr. Humphry, while this was happening, was there or overheard, and Aloysius attacked him?" She snorted and sat back in the cab. "Why would Al do that to Fritz, and then send him to his sisters to recover?"

A slight twitch caught Andrew's lips, and his moustache curled upward on one side before vanishing. He leant forward and levelled his gaze. He was now completely engaged. "Aloysius may not have *meant* to kill your brother. It could have been an accident. Perhaps it was, and he attacked Mr. Humphry for witnessing it all, but couldn't bear to kill another."

Because Al Carlow is a good man.

"It could also be that Miss Murphy refused to let him."

Because Beulah is innocent.

"So Aloysius helps Fritz, and then later when Fritz wakes up, explains the situation. Miss Murphy begs on Al's behalf."

Beulah is innocent but a tad deceitful?

"And Fritz agrees to say nothing, if only because he doesn't wish one tragedy to become a disaster."

See? Everyone's still good. But they did a bad thing. By accident... and are lying about it.

He sat back and crossed his arms and she recognized his curious stare.

You want to know whether I think it's possible that the people you're mentioning could hide Ernie's death from me? Even if they thought it was for the better and it was out of their concern for yours truly?

She didn't know. The instant answer had been no, but then the puzzle seemed to form, and the picture, though grand, made some kind of sense. Beulah would vouch for both men... but would she really hide a secret like that from *her?* It had only been a couple of days. Mayhap Beulah was waiting for things to settle? Ethel shook her head. Was this the best-case scenario?

No. A burglar would be.

A burglar meant that everyone was innocent. "That is *one* theory, Mr. Bertram," Ethel finally replied.

The constable agreed. "I hope to have it expelled by this afternoon. I don't think that's the case."

Ethel nodded at the sincerity of his slight smile. Relieved, of sorts, to know that he didn't truly suspect her family. *Except, perhaps Dolly...*

"I know it's only been a day but have you noticed anything missing at Eden Hall?"

Ethel shook her head, comforted that his suspicions had finally veered towards the best-case scenario.

"I have not been there long, and Dolly had so few maids that it's hard to know what is missing. But... I did find that a brooch of hers was absent from her jewellery collection, though why someone would take that and not the others is questionable." Ethel bit her lip and looked outside beyond the panels flecked in muck. *That brooch from the store looked* exactly *like Dollys... but I saw that brooch there before the murder. Is there a connection?*

Her mind was scrambled and compounded by the tasks she had yet to conquer today, Ethel waved the white flag. She explained to the constable what the brooch looked like, telling him from where it was missing. Bertram agreed it was strange that a thief would take it and leave the rest behind, but perhaps it had been set outside her chambers and the burglar stole it without having to enter her room.

Perhaps there is no burglar. Or there is, he came, and the thing that killed Ernie was still haunting the Hall.

Her stomach heaved, making a sound. Ethel quickly found her kerchief.

"Are you all right, Miss Ethel?" Mr. Bertram asked, leaning forward to offer aid.

Ethel shook her head and swallowed past her panic. "Y-yes, Mr. Bertram. Sorry." She cleared her throat. "Would you mind terribly if we were to change the subject? I'm afraid we are almost there."

It wasn't too much for her. They *were* almost there, and the stinging scent of mud was briny near the water. "Of course, Miss Ethel," he said, tapping his pipe. "And thank you. You've given me much to think about."

Ethel was certain she'd never sleep again. "You're welcome, Constable Bertram."

The coach stopped. He stepped out and offered a hand to help her down. "*Mister Bertram* is fine, if you don't mind, Miss Ethel?"

Ethel smiled and took his hand. "Not at all, Mr. Bertram," she said.

Chapter 14

Mrs. Orla Kennedy lived in a snug little apartment situated in a lot between Water and King Street. It was on the second floor of a barber shop, and the family rented their space from the lovely old man who lived downstairs.

As the coach rode up to the side of the walk, Mr. Bertram observed, with some amusement, that this was the very barber that was recommended to new recruits joining the police force.

"It has a solid reputation," he said with a smile, glancing down towards her before his eyes darted up, towards his hairline. Ethel chuckled, taken aback by the playful mood of her companion. Mr. Bertram always looked so stoic and cold, that the crack in his facade was endearing.

She stifled a laugh behind her palm. "I can see it does, Mr. Bertram," she said, gladdened to be privy to this sudden complexity of his character. As the two made their way upstairs, she was happy to have at least learned a little more about him.

Fritz Humphrey was in the back room of the Kennedy's three-bedroom loft. Orla

Kennedy, who had been home to receive them, did so with her two young sons in tow.

"Aloysius said you'd be coming," Orla said, one son in arm as the other hugged around her skirts. "Your friend's in the back, if you'd follow me." She had long, red hair, plaited into a hasty bun, and her voice spoke of a history across the pond. It was a trait she did not share with her brother, though like Al, Orla was quite handsome.

"We brought you some bread as thanks for caring for our friend."

"Isn't nothing, Miss. Me brother Al helps me out from time to time, and I've no complaint of returning the favour. 'Sides... me boys in bed make more of a fuss than this old man." She smiled in the doorway, peering in then stepping away to allow the other two guests to enter.

Fritz was abed but sitting up with a flannel shirt tossed on around his long johns. He was packing a pipe with tobacco, and the window facing the door was open, looking out towards King Street. There was a little side table next to the bed, and a basin at its foot for washing. The room wasn't big enough for three visitors, so Orla stepped back after pointing to the corner.

"There's a chair over there, if you'd like, though we only have room for the one. I'll bring around some warm tea, and something for *you* to eat later."

Fritz harrumphed, then looked toward Ethel, a bit of a grin in his old, heavy eyes.

"They won't let me leave, Miss Etty. And they force me to eat Irish stew thrice a day."

"Force? You had four helpings on your own yesterday and asked me to bring you more for breakfast!" She glanced towards the guests. "I would 'ave, too, but he'd ate the whole pot yesterday."

Ethel laughed, relieved at the exchange between the woman and Mr. Humphrey. She was glad that Fritz had had the company of people like this, subsequent to the death of her brother. Ethel leant forward and took the young woman by the hand. "Thank you, Mrs. Kennedy," she said with a squeeze, "for your kindness and generosity."

Mrs. Kennedy smiled, and her features warmed as she adjusted her son on her hip and waved away Miss Ethel's kind regard.

"It's nothing at all, Miss. Stay as long as you'd like."

Again, Fritz harrumphed, though Ethel paid him little mind. She walked into the room, her skirts brushing the quilted covers of the bedclothes as she took a seat in the chair beside the nightstand. Constable Bertram came in after her but stood in the doorway to grant a fair amount of space for Ethel.

"I'm so glad you're all right, Fritz. I'm so sorry I didn't come sooner, I—"

He rubbed his fingers together, sprinkling the bit of tobacco left over on a small tin pan that held a pouch and matches. As he popped the unlit pipe in his mouth,

Fritz glanced over at her, and his free hand patted her's.

"Never mind, Miss Etty. We all suffered in those dark days, and when in the dark it's hard to find one another." He lit his pipe.

"At least it's starting to look a little brighter."

Fritz nodded and blew out a breath of smoke. "Just like that time, Miss Etty."

She agreed. It was very much like that time. Only, she felt like if she tried, she may at least spare someone some hurt. In doing so, perhaps she'd help herself and her grief.

"Do you think we both could visit for a while? Constable Bertram is looking into it all if you'd spare some time for him."

Fritz agreed, so long as he could enjoy his pipe. He was regarding the door, and as he gave a slight incline of his head, Mr. Bertram entered and gestured towards the basket of bread.

"Miss Ethel brought you some bread," he indicated, placing it at the foot of the bed after finding no room for it elsewhere.

"Next time, bring whiskey or gin! These folks may say they're Irish, but they're dryer than an old potato."

"I heard that, Mr. Humphry!" Came a call from the kitchen, engulfed by the squeal of her children and the clang of pots and pans.

"Well, then get me a drink!"

"I won't have the devil's nectar in me house. Get better, and you can indulge yourself all you like!"

"Al will come soon. Al will sneak me some," he mumbled with a sniff, blowing out a stream of smoke as though he were a dragon. Ethel chuckled and kept her silence. That was between Al, Fritz, and Mrs. Kennedy, though she was obliged to believe Al and Fritz would quickly regret their conspiracy.

"So... can you tell me, Fritz, what all happened?" Ethel asked.

Fritz hung his head and stared at the stitched squares of the quilt for a moment before nodding. "Aye, Miss Etty. Aye... and I've a few questions of my own, too, if you don't mind. About Dolly."

She sipped in a breath through pursed lips but agreed, straightening her back as they began the exchange. Mr. Bertram stood for a while, listening as the two conversed, but he had retreated once the talk turned from inquiry to a more general nature.

"I'm glad your friend is all right," Bertram said as he helped Ethel board the wagon.

"Me too," Ethel replied with a sigh of relief as she arranged her skirts within the coach. She settled into the seat and drew the wooden window blinds open as Bertram closed the door and moved to bid farewell. The pall hadn't left the city of Charlottetown, but it wasn't raining at the moment.

He paused and seemed to be ruminating as his eyes climbed to meet hers. "After today, I don't believe Fritz Humphrey is implicated in your brother's murder," he whispered, glancing once towards the driver as he leant into the wagon.

"And Al? And Beulah?" she asked with a note of hopeful optimism.

Again, the constable was quiet, and gone was the impish tone he'd harboured when he'd first arrived at the Kennedy's. "I know you are fond of them, especially Miss Murphy, but no, I have yet to remove them from the list of culpable suspects."

Ethel let out the breath she'd been holding and looked away, discouraged by his response. Even if he did rule them all out, there was still Dolly to prove innocent. Ethel wished she had something to add, something that may help to find the culprit quicker.

"You know, I refrained from explaining something before about that brooch. Not through any malicious intent but because I wasn't sure what it meant."

Bertram quirked a brow and tipped his hat forward as the skies released raindrops.

Ethel cleared her throat, thinking if he knew this information and could track it down, it may somehow help dear Beulah and Al Carlow to clear their names.

"The brooch that went missing. I found an exact copy of it at E.W. Taylor's. I... I'm not sure if it's the same one, but I stumbled across it a few days before this all happened.

Miss Murphy was with me at the time, and she came to help find a gift for Dolly. Perhaps," she tried to tie the line of reasoning together. "Perhaps there was a burglar, and he came back for more? After realising that Eden Hall kept many treasures?"

Andrews' eyes regarded her, the robust hickory of his pupils hardening into boiled leather. "That is *one* theory, Miss Arsenault," he said, scratching his chin as he looked back along the thirsty roads yawning with ruts ready to swallow the rain. "Thank you, I'll look into that right away."

He turned on his heel to leave, tapping the side of the wagon to inform the driver that they could depart. Ethel called out to him and lurched as the wagon refrained from its withdrawal.

"Take this," she said, throwing him her umbrella as the mud squelched and the wagon resumed its path forward. She hurried to close the shutters but peeked through the open slates to smile at him. "And please let me know if you find anything more."

She wasn't sure he'd heard her, but as the wagon lumbered down the quagmire that was Water Street, she thought she saw him nod and wave.

"The rain's gonna make these roads a stew! Mind if we just return ya home, Miss?"

Ethel agreed, offering her thanks to the driver before shutting the windows and relaxing back into the darkness of the coach.

A burglar was the best-case scenario... a burglar that came twice to the Hall, however, meant that a burglar could come again.

He could come again and hurt us all...

Ethel closed her eyes, breathing in the brackish scent of mud and salt. She'd think on that later, reprise the theory when she had a moment's grace. Right now, however, she had to get back, go through the files that Ernest had left, and speak with Beulah of Fritz.

"I am not afraid of storms, for I am learning how to sail my ship," she said, listening as the skies fell down around her, and the little wagon creaked and shuddered all the way back to Eden Hall.

Chapter 15

The next few days were filled with relative calm. With the skies continuing to weep upon the soggy roads of Charlottetown, there was less to do but stay around the house. Ethel used most of the time to get Ernest's things in order, but when she craved a break from reality, she'd tuck herself away, up on the third floor with Little Women, and read. The space up there was best at dusk, when the sky blushed red as the moon whispered to it sweet nothings. Oddly enough, it was there she had the fiercest dreams. Dozing on the chaise lounge, exhausted by the day's visits with sympathetic well-wishers and neighbours. Ethel often dreamt of colliding ships, seabed graveyards, and mounds of mud floating with caskets.

Beulah always found her after a while, and arm in arm they'd walk to the second floor until Ethel was abed. It was a great relief to be found and escorted by Beulah. Ethel couldn't imagine waking in the night alone, thinking of burglars and the like while anxiously analysing every little sound she heard as she made her way to her room. But despite the threat of waking alone in the dark, Ethel always found herself back here, watching over the water and reading.

The police, after extensive examination of the body, had returned Ernest's remains to the family. Funeral arrangements needed to be made, and Ethel thought, with some manner of grim amusement, that it was all to be made much easier since she'd been through the same with Roland.

For some matters, she wished Dolly had been there to consult. Small things, like choosing the colour of the flowers for the funeral parlour, or which suit would most favour Ernie's form, were delicate things only his wife would know best. On the other hand, however, Ethel was glad to make the hard choices. Which casket was most preferred? Who should lead the sermon? Where should people be received? Useless questions that were entirely necessary, but also miserable and heart wrenching.

"According to his will, he wants to be buried in Summerside."

"Summerside?" Ethel replied, looking over the desk of papers to where Beulah sat on the other side. "Not in Charlottetown? Where his widow and his businesses are?" Could they take his body back and leave Dolly to mourn without a grave?

Ethel squirmed and bit at her lip. "We need to wait until Dolly has returned before having the funeral, anyway. In the meantime, we can plan for the body to come home to Greens Shore and for there to be a separate ceremony in Charlottetown so people may pay their respects. We should also make sure there is a memorial stone…"

"I'll make a note to inform the mortician."

Beulah nodded and scribbled something on a sheet of paper, before resuming her pile of documents to file. Everywhere smelled of ink and paper, but the scent was becoming tiresome. Both her and Beulah had been working like toy soldiers, mindlessly marching ahead to complete tasks and obligations. Being together made it all easier, but the amount of energy it drew each day gave cause for sleepless nights.

Ethel was constantly hearing sounds. Thumps from the third floor, scratches from the kitchens. Sometimes she'd hear footsteps in the hall while in bed. During the day she also noticed things had gone missing. Liquor, bread, meat from the pantry. Things would be moved all over the house. Cabinets left open, a picture askew, but she thought perhaps Al or Adella were likely the culprits. It was hard to know what liberties Ernest and Dolly had allowed their staff, so Ethel just made note of it, if for nothing else than to help chronicle the days at Eden Hall.

The mud wasn't a creature of mercy. The roads were sopping wet swamps one day, and hungry bogs the next. Winds that hardly blew across a picket fence could topple it if they'd not been buried deep enough, and even the planks of the sidewalks had sunk along the building's hem.

Ethel worried over Dolly and prayed that the poor girl didn't think she had abandoned her. There was so much Ethel wanted to ask her about. So much more she wanted to *know*.

Constable Bertram came around a few times, often just to check on her, but a few days after their initial meeting, he'd arrived to tell her that the brooch had gone missing. "Dolly said the brooch was lost."

"Lost? When?" Ethel asked, her tea ignored as they sat in Ernest's now-tidied den.

"Sometime after you'd arrived at Eden Hall." Andrew Bertram seemed lost in the scent of the perking tea for a moment. With his eyes closed, he took a sip before setting it down on the saucer in his palm. "She wasn't sure how or where she'd lost it, but I figure it *could* have been stolen. If so, someone could have pawned it off for cash. The store you mentioned—" he said when he failed to recall its name.

"E.W. Taylor's?"

"Yes. The owner there confirmed it had been pawned a few days prior." He reached into his pocket and withdrew a velvet box trimmed in gold embroidery. Ethel's eyes glazed over when he opened it to reveal the silver and garnet brooch Dolly had worn the first night Ethel had arrived at Eden Hall.

How could she have lost it? Ethel wondered, taking the box and smiling into the light that shined from its garnet clusters. *Dolly hadn't worn it to dinner that night, at the Windmill. And every day after, she had stayed at home sick.*

"Did he recall who pawned it?" Ethel asked, her fingers twitching as her hands rung together.

Bertram shook his head and pinched at his top lip in an anxious apology. "He couldn't recall finding him familiar."

"He could have been a sailor," she said.

"If so, the sailors have all gone, Miss Ethel. The last few ships left for Boston the very day your brother was found. If a burglar came into Eden Hall, *twice,* and killed Ernest, it's likely they've already left via boat."

The best-case scenario was that the killer got away...

Ethel hung her head and peered across the polished tabletop. She tapped at the saucer with her fingers, chewed at her inner cheek, all signs to just *stop thinking* and carry onward. But how well *did* she know everyone at Eden Hall? How much did she know Al, or Adella, or even Dolly?

She didn't, really. *But I do know Ernie... and Ernie was always a good judge of character.*

"I have to tell you, Miss Ethel, that I do have one theory, and as of late, it is becoming more and more plausible."

She picked her head up.

"Do you think it could be possible that Dolly had a lover?" He took another drink of tea, and across the room, the mantlepiece gonged at six o'clock. It startled her, the sound, the implication, the talk of adultery... and as he held her eyes ransom, Ethel inhaled and looked away.

Her first inclination had been to say no. But then, Dolly was so sweet... Ethel wondered if someone could have taken advantage of her?

"I don't know," she replied, realising too late how that sounded. "I mean!—I don't think so... I-I won't admit to knowing Dolly very well, but do I know that there was love between her and my brother."

The constable nodded and glanced towards the office door. "I understand, and I hope I've not offended you, Miss Arsenault."

She frowned but shook her head. "No. Of course not. I—I understand, but—"

"There was no evidence of anyone entering or leaving the house. If it was a lover..."

Something seemed to light in his eyes, and for a brief moment, he looked like a starved man who'd felt a nibble at the end of his fishing line. So eager was his gaze, that Ethel was prompted to follow it to the door and out towards the foyer.

"Is something the matter, Mr. Bertram?" she asked, panic welling in her chest at the alarm within his eyes.

He snapped straight, like a lad who'd been struck with a paddle. "I'm sorry, Miss Ethel, I—I thought I saw something in the corner of my eye."

Her mind was a moth, charred in the fire. "What do you mean? No one is here."

He looked abashed and lost for words. Leaning forward to surrender his cup, he peered at her, *about to change the subject,* she thought. "Miss Ethel, do you think I could call on you tomorrow?"

"Why?" What had he seen? *What had happened in the space of a single second?* Ethel paused, her eyes stinging from the avid stare she was levelling upon the constable.

He was gazing at a halo that hovered on the top of Ernest's desk. The moon behind her, shining through the office window, struck his face and made him pale. "Well... It's already late. I'm certain a lady of your calibre must go to bed early and sleep in until noon."

She was struck off guard and sent reeling. Ethel could only blink back as he stood up and grabbed his coat to leave. "W-what?" she asked, not sure if she ought to be offended. She scrambled to follow him, almost tripping over the tabletop in an effort to get around it fast enough.

"Tomorrow, there is an early supper at my church. It's not far from here, and there are to be a great number of individuals who were acquainted with Ernest. I know rumours like to run amok, and thought perhaps if you were to accompany me, they may see you and be…" he was grasping the den's door handle but paused as though to toss the words around like candy in his mouth, "*rest assured* that the members of Eden Hall are coping well."

Coping? Is that what she was doing? She must have been. What else was there to do? But coping *well?* If Ethel went with him, then Charlottetown would see Ernie's sister. Perhaps those ill at ease with Dolly's innocence could hear Ethel's confidence in her and be assured of her guiltlessness.

"All right, Mr. Bertram," she said as he was stepping out the door. Her reply gave him pause, and he stopped upon the threshold.

"The members of Eden Hall *are* coping well, right, Miss Ethel?"

She looked up at his inquiry, startled by his concern. As her shock evaporated into something comforting and warm, Ethel smiled down at the heavy planks of the rain drenched porch. "It's hard to tell, but I think so. Thank you, Mr. Bertram, for your concern."

He nodded and tipped his chin to keep his lips concealed beneath his moustache. "Then go and get your beauty sleep, Miss Ethel," he said, moving down the stairs towards the path. The lamplighters were late, postponed by the constant rain, and so as he went, she saw the darkness of the lawn, crowned in the lace of roiling ocean waves.

For a moment, Ethel's vision blurred, and looking out the door, all there was before her was the black belly of the sea, swallowing a man.

Her mouth was open to call out to him, but the flash of panic ebbed, and though images of Roland fluttered in her mind, they tumbled like photos to settle in the album of her heart.

"That I may dazzle the natives, to-morrow..." Ethel whispered, shutting the door to lean against it.

What did you see, Mr. Bertram? She looked at her hands. They were shaking, and for the first time, Ethel noticed how thin and knobby they'd gotten. She hugged herself as the air grew cold, and a shiver ran up her spine.

Did Dolly have a lover? *How possibly could she? Ernest was gone so much... Did she get lonely?*

Ethel had come here at Ernest's request for that very reason. Had she arrived too late?

Who's to blame? What if it really was a burglar, and we'll never know why or how they did it?

Could *she* accept the best-case scenario?

"Are you coming upstairs, Miss Ethel? I thought we'd wash your hair tonight," Beulah called from upstairs, and the sound was like a bell tolling

The grandfather clock rang nine from the second floor. It was a few seconds off from the gong of the mantlepiece.

"Yes. Thank you, and if you'd like, perhaps we could share a glass or two of gin?"

Beulah made a face but smiled to show her support "If you think you need it, Miss Ethel. We can make a toast to Ernest... But make sure to mix mine with lots of lime. Never knew how Ernie did it, drinking it neat like he did."

Ethel chuckled. Glad for Beulah's presence. Glad not to be *lonely* as she wandered up to bed for the night.

Chapter 16

It didn't matter what she wore because it would be black. That's all the people expected. Nothing too extravagant, but something minimal to exemplify the mourner's inability to function beyond anything other than what propriety deemed tolerable.

It wasn't hard because neither she nor Beulah had much energy for anything else. They had awoken that morning in Ethel's bed. An empty bottle of gin and two glasses rolled around between them on the blankets.

Beulah was snoring, her face pressed into the pillow, her bun unpinned as Ethel got up and rummaged through the wardrobe. Black dress, shoes—a sturdy pair for the roads, and a jacket. She grabbed a box, too, and opened it. Inside were the matching pair of swallow brooches, the ones she meant to gift to Dolly and to Ernest.

She pinned one against her throat, and when it came time for Constable Bertram to escort her to supper, she tied her hair with a ribbon. Ethel was mourning, but she was also fighting for her sister. That the constable was helping her, keeping her informed, was of great comfort, if only because it kept her on task as she began the climb from her basement of misery.

It wasn't a whirlwind affair, but a dinner of good cheer wrapped in sad circumstances. The church was contemporary, a brand new edition to the community that had yet to be consecrated. As such, it was used more as a meeting place and situated in a community named West Bog just northeast of Eden Hall. Despite its relative proximity to the affluent West Street, West Bog was an area of Charlottetown known to be disreputable amongst the other residents of the city.

"By building the church there, they hope to establish the community better and maybe erect a few governmental buildings in the future," Bertram explained.

Ethel was glad to see that the state of the roads had improved and hoped she'd be able to visit Dolly with encouraging news, after a day or two.

The church was tall, the rectangular narthex of the would-be cathedral standing high ahead of the inner nave. It was buttressed on each side by squat towers with two thin, arched windows. A circle of stained glass let in light through the facade of the building towards the rear chapel. Already, men and women were commingling inside where the pews would have been had it been a working church. Some attendees she remembered seeing before were men from the Windmill that had caroused with her brother. Others were women and gentlemen from the greater community of Charlottetown. Politicians, landowners, lawmakers. Mr. Bertram named them all, and now, away from the scent of mud and horses, she realised that the suit he wore was the same as the night they had attended the Windmill. Though it was missing the scent of dust.

"I'm so sorry for—"

"My condolences Miss—"

"I heard she was having an affair..."

Amidst the constant sympathies that were swept at Ethel whenever she'd approach, beneath the surface of the luncheon were angry rumours and baseless accusations that seemed intent on demonising poor Dolly.

"Perhaps that's why Ethel came on Ernest's behest."

"Maybe he couldn't trust her anymore."

Ethel listened with climbing concern, saying a good word when she could but shying away from confrontation. Even as she defended Dolly's innocence, she could hear the idle scorn and gossip of those in suspicion around her. Ethel was astounded by the public's opinion of Ernest's new wife. Dolores Arsenault was young. She was a social butterfly, pretty, rich, and often left alone.

"She *must* have had a lover."

"But who? I've heard the police have found no evidence..."

Because there is no one. Dolly wouldn't do that. Dolly was a happy girl. Right?

Ethel closed her eyes, rubbing at her temples as the holy saints adorning the sanctuary bounced in the light of the outdoors. The sun caught on the golden skies of the frescos and illuminated the tawny belly of St. Peter's would-be cathedral. It hurt Ethel's eyes and caused her hands to shake.

"Are you all right, Miss Ethel?" Bertram asked an hour after six. The weather was pleasant, yet the quality of the day's events had worn a crease upon her brow.

"Do you mind if we take a walk, Mr. Bertram? I'm afraid I'm feeling... out of sorts."

They went outside, and for once in a long time, Ethel smelled the grass. Across the way, beyond Government Pond, north of West Street, she saw the sun spackled back of rapeseed fields, sprouting in banks of gold. The mud in the streets was drying, and she wondered if being bundled indoors too long had left the people of Charlottetown cruel and starved for gossip.

"I'm sorry, Miss Ethel," Bertram said as they walked aside the Rochford Square gardens. "I didn't realise... many of those attending were quite fond of your brother. Ernest was a pillar, and his presence will be missed."

"Everyone blames Dolly. Everyone thinks that she killed Ernie." *Am I so naive?*

Bertram's silence revealed his mind as he tried to piece together some words of comfort. "The investigation is still underway. It would be best if you did not let public opinion weigh you down with worry."

"How can it not? Dolly's been arrested, ferried away to Falconwood. How can the public not see her terribly, when the authorities are holding her in a mental asylum? There's been no evidence of a lover. You've torn apart Eden Hall, yet you've found no apple and no bite."

She missed the smell of dust. Around them the skies were a cool, bruised purple that had bled from black to tangerine. The clouds hung to the colours like brushstrokes, and the noisome caws of gulls came from houses on the far banks of West Street.

They turned the corner. Eden Hall was up ahead. Its plum, cross gabled roof basked in the final, wounded rays of sunlight.

"I don't understand, Mr. Bertram, why you've shared so much with me, yet won't defend my sister's innocence."

"It's all quite complicated, Miss Ethel." He looked down, fetched a pipe that had been stowed in his pocket, and cleaned the bowl. "I don't want to alarm you, but out of everyone, I *know* you are innocent. This is why I've shared so much, and also because—"

Beulah, Dolly, Al and Fritz. Why only me?

His reluctance to answer was crumbling in the wake of her gaze as he looked towards the waiting hall. His eyes widened, caught at something peculiar, and as Andrew pocketed his pipe, half filled with tobacco, Al bounded towards them.

"Miss Ethel! Miss Ethel, get away. There's someone in the house!"

"What?" There was a faint smell of liquor as she took a step forwards. Beulah was behind him, her skirts in her hands in an effort to keep from tripping.

"Miss Ethel, you shouldn't go in! There's been another break in—"

"Are you certain there is someone inside?" Ethel swung her head to glance at Mr. Bertram. She was startled to see him carrying a pistol.

"If they ain't inside, they ain't long gone." Al puffed, hands on his knees as he stood straight and watched the constable pass.

"Where are you going, Mr. Bertram?" Ethel cried, following after until he paused.

"Stay here, Miss Arsenault! I'll go take a look."

Ethel inhaled and grasped at the silver swallow pinned at the base of her throat. As Beulah stepped to Ethel's side, Al bounded back towards the hall. He stopped when the constable held out his hand in a wordless reproach.

"Shouldn't we alert someone?" Ethel asked, taking Beulah by the hand to keep herself from following him.

"I—I don't know." There was a faint smell of liquor in the air, and Al—running his hands through his mop of blondish curls—turned to address the ladies, stumbling a bit as he swung around.

"My shotgun's in the stable. You ladies stay here. I'm gonna go lend a hand."

"But the constable said we should *all* stay here!" Beulah shouted, watching as Aloysius turned to sprint towards the barn. "Miss Ethel, what do we do?"

I don't know.

Ethel stood, quiet in the street as the sun tucked itself beneath the island's coast. She saw the lights go on inside, lighting up as someone went from room to room. Without the blaze of the setting sun, the cool wind licked up her neck without shame. The neighbourhood was dark, the lamplighter late or lost as the chorus of crickets began singing the night's melody.

"We should go in!"

"Shh! Look, Beulah. Someone's coming."

His coat was inhaling the sudden change of the wind, and as it gulped, Ethel noticed a holster beneath Constable Bertram's arm.

"I'm sorry to keep you waiting, ladies. You can come inside."

"Is everything all right?" Ethel marched up to meet him, her arm looped around

Beulah's as she held the poor woman's shaking hand.

Bertram gestured to the house and motioned for them to make haste. "We'll talk inside. Come, where it's warm."

The gas lights were lit in the foyer, the chains that controlled their radiance pulled down as far as they'd go. A box of half-used matches sat upon the stair railing, though the chandelier that hung from the second floor landing remained unlit.

Al was in the sitting room off the left hand side of the main entry. He was stoking the fire, his shotgun leaning next to the dining table where Ethel had often taken breakfast with Dolly and her brother.

"Beul—ah, Miss Murphy, Miss Ethel... we uh, whoever it was seemed to have got away."

"Mr. Carlow, was it?" Bertram asked, his gun stowed and replaced with his pipe as he motioned for the women to have a seat. He waited until Al had nodded before continuing, "Why don't you run a kettle for the ladies. I'm sure they'd appreciate something to warm themselves up."

Ethel let her eye wander down Al's back as he left to oblige the grave-faced constable. There was a subtle glance shared between Al and Beulah, and Ethel wondered if there was something else afoot when she and the constable had returned.

Andrew sat down.

He's occupying the same chair he did when he'd questioned Dolly. This time however, it was her and Beulah on the sofa. Not Dolly.

Mr. Bertram sighed, steepling his fingers between his legs as he leant forward and glanced up through tired eyes. "Can you tell me exactly what happened, Miss Murphy?" he asked.

Beulah gulped, looking this way and that before nodding. "I was coming home from shopping. Al Carlow was helping me, on account of the roads. When we came in, we saw someone on the stairs."

"Did Mr. Carlow not investigate?" Bertram asked, studying her like a book about to disintegrate.

Beulah shook her head. "He wanted to, but I held him back. I didn't want a repeat of... what happened before," she stopped, and studied his reaction before Bertram nodded, and she continued, "We didn't know what to do. Al was going to go get his shotgun when we saw you coming down the road. I— I don't think he knew who you were until he was up close, but I think he was looking for someone to come help."

"And you said this all happened after coming back from shopping?"

Ethel peeked over at Beulah as her friend's grip tightened upon her arm.

"That's right," she replied looking towards the set of doors that led back into the foyer.

"So, you opened the door, and *then* you saw the intruder at the top of the stairs?"

"Mr. Bertram, I don't think I understand your line of questioning," Ethel replied, cross to see her friend so anxious. She stood up and offered Miss Murphy a hand. "Why don't I take you upstairs to bed? You're positively shaken, and I doubt all the hot tea in the world would do you good right now." Ethel had never seen Beulah so out of sorts.

"But the man—"

"There is nobody here, Miss Murphy," Bertram said to the dining room carpet. He leant back into his seat as though he was set to stay awhile. "Your friend Al and I made certain, but I'll stay downstairs, just to give you peace of mind."

Ethel was relieved, though the sentiment didn't seem to assuage Beulah's trembling nerves. "I'll come back up and stay with you after he's gone," Ethel whispered as they approached the steps.

"Oh Miss Ethel, I didn't mean—I shouldn't have gone out with Al."

Ethel patted her on the shoulder, realising the cause of Beulah's distress. "Don't be silly. Come, let's get you to bed."

It was a strange relief to be able to help her friend, and for once, as the two went upstairs, Ethel forgot to look in all the dark spaces. *Do I feel safer because of Al, or because Mr. Bertram is downstairs and he said there was no intruder?* Or did she feel sage because she didn't think a ghost would have the energy to appear twice in one night.

Could it have been a ghost?

It was absurd, but as Ethel helped Beulah dress for bed, she tried to rationalise her reasoning. *The possibility is slim by a logical standpoint, but if they both had seen a character at the top of the stairs, where could that person have run off to?* The servant's halls led back downstairs, but if Al had come into Eden Hall from the barn, then wouldn't he have met the intruder?

Ethel came back downstairs a little while later. Mr. Bertram still sat in the same chair, a tray of hot tea on the table in front of him. There were two cups, one already in use, and a small pot. The fire had died down somewhat, and the long window that framed the breakfast nook in the back had been opened to let in a scant bit of the evening breeze.

"I find it difficult to believe that those two went out shopping yet brought nothing back with them." He turned to watch her as she entered and then bent to pour her some tea as Ethel sat upon the sofa.

"Have you been down here ruminating the whole time?" she asked, smiling to remove the bite from her words. She looked back towards the foyer and picked up her cup to drink. "Where is Mr. Carlow?"

"I told him he could retire for the night." Bertram had his legs crossed and a hand upon his ankle. His fingers were tapping at the pattern of his argyle socks, while his other hand scratched at his chin. "He was a bit out of sorts. I assume he had drank too much."

Ethel frowned and set her cup down before she had the chance to drink from it. "Mr. Bertram, I know you suspect them, but please... They haven't been seeing each other for long, and I'm certain they've been reluctant to say anything with everything that has happened." She filled her lungs, glad to see that he was looking at her and paying her mind. She continued, "People would talk if they knew Mr. Carlow was courting Beulah so soon after Ernest's—" she hesitated to say it. The wound was still raw. "But in fact, I think they took a liking to each other during the ride from Summerside."

"Miss Ethel, do you know why I never suspected you?"

For the murder of my brother? When it came to such terrible affairs, she supposed an officer would have reason to suspect everyone.

"No. Why?"

He took in a deep breath and uncrossed his leg, leaning forward with both elbows on his knees. "Because I believe you were poisoned."

Ethel made a face. "What? How?"

"On the morning of Ernest's death, you were roused with the scent of pears on your breath... a telling sign of chloral hydrate."

"Chloral—"

"It's usually used as a treatment for insomnia. I saw a vial of it in the kitchens, next to the spirits and alcohol. A few vials, actually, some empty and reused for storage purposes." He paused, steepling his fingers before bridging them together and glancing back up at her. "One theory I have is that Beulah tampered with your drink. You said you had been drinking heavily with Mrs. Arsenault the evening before, correct?"

Ethel nodded.

"So, it's possible that your serving girl poisoned you, perhaps on Mr. Carlow's behalf. In fact, when you were found upstairs, she admitted that she thought you'd been poisoned. Did she do it because she was seeing Mr. Carlow in secret at the time?"

They had been seeing each other. Beulah told me afterwards. After Ernest's death.

"I don't see why that means that they are responsible for murder."

Bertram leant away, and his gaze wandered towards the window. "I believe Dolores Arsenault was having an affair... and I also believe that Aloysius Carlow was the man she was having the affair with." He swallowed, as though expecting an interruption, but when none came, Constable Bertram continued, "Al Carlow was always around. He had access to the gun cabinet, and his presence in the house would have been natural. He was also of a similar age to Dolores."

They were both very handsome... also.

"Ernest Arsenault was murdered upstairs after arriving home. No sign of break-in implies that the murderer was already in the house and had a relatively easy time entering it. Dolly was an... avid lady. A young woman prone to charm and conversation. It is not unlikely that she was lonely from Mr. Arsenault's constant absence. An affair with Mr. Carlow is not far-fetched."

Not far-fetched? Is that how a case is solved? How far-fetched is the presence of a ghost?

"On the night of the murder, Ernest comes home. He catches his wife with Aloysius Carlow, and a scuffle occurs, where Ernest is shot dead by his own gun. It is possible he retrieved the gun himself when he heard a commotion upstairs, but I suspect that either way, Mr. Carlow killed your brother on the stairs."

"This commotion alerted Beulah Murphy, who had been waiting for Al to visit her. She was probably unaware of the affair but had used the chloral hydrate earlier in the evening in the hopes of a nightly tryst with her new beau. Of course, none of this occurs because Al runs off after the murder takes place, and Dolly covers for him. It is possible that Beulah knows now, after the fact, but is helping Mr. Carlow for the exchange of affection."

"Why haven't you arrested them?"

He stopped, and the hard lines of his face became sharp as his eyes stared at her with all the intensity of a lion. It was a considering gaze, one of a predator appraising another. Was she an equal? Can Ethel Arsenault handle all the details of this case or should she be locked out, protected, before the lions of truth could hurt her?

Ethel stared back at him until her eyes were glossy. He nodded and broke the gaze, inhaling through his nose as he tried to snuff the smile from his features.

"We need to find the murder weapon. Without it, we can't justify an arrest. There isn't *enough* evidence against Al Carlow."

"Dolly hasn't said anything?"

His eyes returned to hers, and his stoicism was restored. "Nothing. Though if she were to admit to an affair, it would obviously help us immensely." His jaw flexed. "Have you visited her yet?"

Would she admit it to me? That's what you're really asking, isn't it, Mr. Bertram?

Ethel looked at the floor, her nails digging crescent trenches in the back of her right hand.

You're suggesting my entire family is at fault for my brother's murder. Do you understand that, Constable? You're marking everyone responsible and hoping that my love for Ernie will hold me steady as you share the investigation and the theories with me. Out of respect. Because, for some reason, I have garnered that, at least.

"Due to the weather, I've been unable to travel to Falconwood. I was hoping the mud had hardened enough that I may venture out tomorrow. Mr. Carlow has promised to take me."

The silence between them grew like a beach at low tide. Ethel was empty, her mind swept clean by the rush of emotions that she'd pushed away. Mr. Bertram, unsettled in the deafening quiet, looked as though he wanted to reach out, and had reached a hand towards her before his fingers crumpled and his arm arched back to rub at his jaw.

"What about the man in the house?" Ethel asked, smiling at her own attempt to grasp at straws. "The one Mr. Carlow and Miss Murphy saw earlier tonight?"

Mr. Bertram scoffed, though the sound was ruth and without venom. "The liquor cabinet was open when I first entered the house. Probably they'd imagined it."

Because they aren't trustworthy. Because they had gone out shopping and hadn't brought anything back. You won't put weight in their words because their words have been false before.

It made sense, and yet, her sensibilities were overwhelming her. "Maybe Eden Hall is haunted, Mr. Bertram."

"Miss Arsenault?"

There's a question in your eyes, Mr. Bertram. It's asking if I'm all right, if I need to lay down and rest. I do...

"Apologies," she chuckled. "I just wish it *were* the case, because then... everyone I love would not be implicated in my dear brother's death." *Loneliness, thy name is Ethel.* "Though... unless the ghost confessed to its crime—and ghosts do not exist, of course," she added with a glance, "I supposed it would be worse to blame the supernatural and always question, always *know* that there is a chance that someone you love killed someone else you loved. Understanding helps us heal."

Roland had been lost at sea. He was dead. But hope tormented her every day.

She looked at the door. Roland would not come through it, yet, she sustained the hope that he would.

Ethel stood, and in so doing, Mr. Bertram stood as well. "Why don't you go home and rest, Constable."

"Miss Ethel?" He seemed taken aback.

"You don't need to look over us. No one is here." She smiled. "You so said yourself. Thank you for the evening, and I thank you for considering my brother first in all of this."

I may be suffering, but my brother suffered worse. Remember?

She sniffed, and pausing in her endeavour to reassure him, Ethel reached towards his arm, meaning to touch him, when her body gave out, and she collapsed onto the solid surface of his chest. Ethel had nothing, no one, but weeping upon his coat, she was reassured by the scant scent of dust that had kicked up beneath her cheek.

What did it matter? She wept, her emotions freeing her from propriety as she took comfort in his presence, in his form. Andrew was there, and though his body tensed, and his arms were frozen at his sides, there was a war within him. A man, fighting a battle of good manners and civility. He wanted to hold her, but his affections for her kept him from jeopardising her dignity.

This was the definition, the mind of the constable Andrew Bertram. But as his arms finally enveloped her, and his chin tucked to kiss the crown of her head, Ethel found that she was surprised, relieved, and grateful of her false assumptions.

"I'm sorry, Miss Ethel."

It hurt a little less now, if only because as he held her, and she sobbed without consequence, Ethel was able to pour her emotions like debris within the tide.

Thank you, Mr. Bertram. For the depths of your compassion.

In comparison, the sea didn't seem so deep anymore...

...and Ethel didn't mind falling into it...

Chapter 17

Mr. Bertram left in the morning, before Ethel or Beulah had the chance to wake. His insistence on staying and keeping sigil over her, had been, as he put it, an offer of goodwill.

"Assuage my worry that you're not all right and allow me to stay down here in the sitting room." So, Ethel had, and she had slept well.

Which wasn't a coincidence. Mr. Bertram was of a great comfort to her. He treated her like an equal, not a vase that was always in jeopardy of breaking. He didn't seem to mind a crack or chip, understood that everything can break sometimes, and that everything had the potential for mending.

Still, it was hard to face the truths he pursued. *Could everyone I love be to blame?*

Ethel wasn't sure, but despite how much she suffered from the inevitable conclusion of her brother's homicide, she knew she'd heal better knowing the truth, than never knowing anything at all.

Downstairs was cold and quiet when Ethel had emerged from her bedroom. The sun was pouring through the gaps in the curtains, and she gasped at its ferocity as she pulled them aside to see the day. Spring flowers were blooming in the fields and in the shrubs around the house. They tossed their heads to a playful breeze and released their scent to spiral among the elder pines. The roads of Charlottetown were healing. The hardened mud, a bandage for the tumult of rain they had been having, was less a havoc and more operable. In fact, as her eyes adjusted and focused on the periphery of the bay window, she noticed several wagons and coaches already making use of the day's pleasant weather as they rolled on behind the gallop of once-bored horses.

Ethel wanted to be excited for today, the weather, and her trip... but as she dressed, ate, and arranged for the coach, a knot of dread was building in her belly. It tumbled like a wild instrument, tangling into a ball that hung at her heart.

Ethel loved Dolly, but she had loved Ernest longer. Ethel had a brother long before she had a sister-in-law, and despite her affections, she couldn't shake the feeling that Dolly may have been responsible for his death.

Ethel held out hope that their meeting today would shed light on what had happened. *Perhaps, Roland will come through the door today.* Perhaps, she'd get her answer.

So, Ethel prepared and brought her book in case she wished to read a few chapters along the way. She thought it could be a welcome distraction from the flurry of thoughts that raged like mad tornadoes in her mind. But, the book had remained inside her Gladstone bag for the entire trip.

Could Al have killed her brother? Had an affair with Dolly? Manipulated Beulah? Was she being ferried to Hell by the Devil himself?

Aloysius was singing a tune as they went, chirping about the good weather and saying a hearty hello to any passers-by. Could his mirth be a clue? Or a desperate mask made to hide his guilt?

She hated the suspicion that had taken asylum in her mind.

"Are ya in there, Miss Ethel?"

She blinked and saw the avid sparks of light catching in the waves flicker black as voids behind her eyes. "Y-yes. Sorry, I— What were you saying, Aloysius?"

"We're just coming up to Falconwood, Miss Ethel." He was chewing on tobacco and spat it into the ditch as the coach crested the small knoll that had been the prelude to the hospital's main driveway.

It was a sprawling palace, complete with a compound of small farmhouses that likely belonged to the staff. The homes were scattered about the twelve acre lot and hooked together with a thin line of roads made simply by the passage of time and travellers.

The imposing five story structure of Falconwood was in the style of the second empire. Decorated with iron cresting, Falconwood was topped with a tower, making it look like a gateway into another world. Its harsh lines, obsessively symmetrical motifs, and rigid stature stood as guard to its own majesty.

It must have been the most substantial brick building on the island. Certainly, it was the most grand Ethel had ever seen. But as they drew closer, passing a few fine old trees, flower gardens, and a flourishing kitchen garden, the grandiose construct—like a hardened soldier returning from home—had a melancholy to it. Dutiful and proud, but with trauma so heavy they were monsters in the mind. Falconwood Hospital was a wretched man dressed for war.

Dolly was inside here. Somewhere... perhaps looking out one of the forty-eight windows that spanned a single floor of the building's length. There were too many windows for Ethel to count, and yet as she held her hat and peered outside the stagecoach, she tried to look at every one, in hopes of seeing Dolly first.

She was jerked back into her seat as they stopped at the foot of the building's stoop. Mr. Carlow had climbed off from the front and opened her door before she had the chance to mask her worry. Was Dolly all right? Would she admit to wrongdoings?

Had Dolly sat here, resenting her for not coming sooner?

"Are you all right, Miss Ethel?"

She looked up, and her bottom lip trembled as she studied the boyish features of Al Carlow. *Was it really you who killed my dear Ernie? Is that what Dolly is hiding for you?* Ethel nodded at him and took his hand as he held it out for her. *Will she admit that to me? Today? Will I ride home to Eden Hall with the man who murdered my brother?*

Ethel hurried up the stairs, wiping her hand on the front of her skirts to erase the touch of her driver. His palms had been wet, sweating from the leather of the reins, and it had unsettled her. Ethel had gained the stoop and was reaching for the door when she heard Al behind her.

"Tell Dolly we're all... I mean, I'm—"

Ethel turned, snapping like a trout to a lure. Al had his hat in his hand, and he was scuffing a foot, his eyes downcast. "Tell her we're all thinking of her, won't you?"

Ethel wanted to cry, if only because she'd hate to hate this seemingly lovely young man.

Nodding to him and smiling despite herself, Ethel watched him wander off to guide the coach somewhere suitable whilst he waited for her. Stooping to rummage through her Gladstone, Ethel rifled with her things, juggling her journal in her left hand as she grasped a piece of coal in her right.

She scribbled down a sketch—of a man walking with a horse to the fields: his straw hat, rolled-up cuffs, and suspenders, his trousers tucked into riding boots, and the piece of weed that often flicked out the corner of his angled mouth.

Ethel wanted to remember him. Aloysius Carlow. The man she knew before…

Before he—well… in all probability…

Before he became the man who killed my brother.

There was a sense of fondness in the drawing that Ethel thought she'd never replicate if Al was proven to be guilty. She supposed she ought to draw the others as well, and the thought caused her to stiffen and put her book away.

You've already decided they're guilty, Etty. Even Beulah, who you've known since childhood. Why?

Because I'm sick of hoping. Ethel stared forwards at the heavy door that led inside the Falconwood Asylum. She was willing herself to see through it. *I'm sick of hoping for him on the other side. I'm sick of hoping for that small chance!*

She barrelled through it, almost tripping over the threshold before colliding with a nurse on the other side.

"I'm so sorry!" the nurse yelped as both women began collecting themselves. "I was just coming to greet you."

Ethel shook her head, dazed for a moment, before realising her mistake.

"No, no, please. It's my fault, I—I shouldn't have burst in like that."

The nurse smiled and fixed her hair. She was an older woman, stout like a barn, and dressed in a brown frock. "The fault is mine. We were just taking a group picture," she waved a hand behind her, "and had to sit still for the exposure time."

The room was brightly lit, made so by the long front windows and sidelights that hovered near the door. Though the first few feet inside were within the large rectangular vestibule, at the back of the room a hall swept. It was a good ten feet wide, like a galley with doors that lined its flanks in perfect symmetry and was more than sixty feet long. A group of women sat along the length of it, in wooden beach chairs with blankets across their laps. A few young nurses prattled on with the residents and regarded their guest at the door, shawls about their shoulders and white aprons tied at their waists.

"The camera won't take the picture properly if we do not sit still, and getting all the residents to be seated is no easy task." The nurse laughed, including Ethel in her mirth as she led her from the door.

The hallway was chilly, like a mausoleum, and already a few patients were heading back inside their rooms, where the temperature was better moderated.

"Do you want a blanket, Miss? It gets terribly cold here, and heating the halls of the Nest is a fool's errand." Seemingly sensing Ethel's thoughts, the nurse bent to retrieve a folded wool blanket to wrap about Ethel's shoulders before she could protest. "Usually we keep the main areas and the bedrooms warm for the residents, but we wanted to take a picture and the light is best through here. We had to bundle up."

"The Nest?" Ethel sputtered, wandering after the nurse who set towards deconstructing the accordion-like camera system.

"Oh," the woman waved her hand. "That's just what we call this place. Falconwood. The Nest..."

"And all the squawking hens inside it?"

The woman laughed and hauled out a box from the left wall. An older man, of a relative age to the nurse but with a portly belly and salt in his beard, moved out from a room at the back of the hall. He picked up the camera and placed it in the box, offering another smile to Ethel as the nurse clapped her hands.

"You mind yourself, Constable Yates! All the way to the back room where you can put this away as an apology, in fact." She kicked the box towards him and waved him away as he chuckled and began to object.

"Sorry. These men have been trying to distract us ever since they arrived a few days ago. Let's go into one of the sitting rooms. It will be much more comfortable there, and we can talk uninterrupted."

"Until the sun goes down, ya mean. Hope your coachmen has all day to waste!" The constable moseyed down the hall in a blithe effort to escape the woman's stare.

It at least seems like a good place, but...

"I'm sorry. I was told by Constable Bertram that I was allowed to see Dolly Arsenault. I'm her sister-in-law. She's here, right?" There was a change in the woman's features, like a cloud had been drawn over the sun. Falconwood grew colder.

"Oh," the woman said, looking about towards the patients still gathering into their rooms and the nurses assisting them. Like a sudden storm had appeared at her tea party, the woman's expression filled with worry.

"W-well..." There was no one else to turn to, otherwise, the woman would have tried to hand her off.

With no effort to conceal it, the nurse sighed and picked up her skirts. She nodded, sparing a glance to Ethel before pointing down the hall. "Follow me." Her command broached no argument, and spinning on her heel like a ballerina, the woman was off.

Ethel followed, letting the gap between them grow as the nurse rushed away. There were a few whispers and pitiable looks from the staff as Ethel tried to maintain a facade of nonchalance, but as they passed, an old woman in a chair spoke up, which caused an uproar amongst the other patients.

"Don't worry dear, they'd never hang a woman."

Ethel jerked to a stop as her head snapped to regard the poor lady. She was in a simple frock with slippers, though her hair had been combed and curled most likely for the photograph. Her lined face was stored of sunspots and the spidery flush of age, though there was a manner of childishness to the old woman that defied her filmy white eyes.

"E-excuse me?" Ethel held a hand to her chest, as though in an attempt to quell her heart.

The nurse who'd been in charge of the patient, gasped as her charge reached forward in an effort to take Ethel's hand. "Betty, be quiet!"

The woman smiled. The press of her fingers was slight, like four candy drops settling in the palm of Ethel's hand.

"They are *all* saying she's to be hanged, but they won't hang a woman," she said the last four words apart from one another, as though to nail the notion home.

The worried gaze of the resident's fretting nurse, standing in the doorway, almost spoiled the sweet lady's sincerity.

Ethel let her gaze linger on the hope in the mad woman's eyes. She nodded, clinging on to the lady's words even though the sane thought otherwise. "Thank you."

"Please, don't pay her *any* mind—" the young caretaker interjected as she attempted to stand in front of her patient. The nurse placed a hand upon Betty's arm, as though signalling that she needed to let go.

The woman did not. Instead, she leant forward. "Even if the trial is short, Dear." She waited until Ethel nodded again, then petted the top of her hand. "The court will never," she shook her head and leant back as though to rock in her chair, "*never* hang a woman." She was shaking her head, rocking back and forth in her foldable beach chair as the nurse stepped wholly between Ethel and her charge.

"Sorry, Miss. She's..."

"They're all mad here." Ethel looked back at the older nurse she'd met at the entrance. The lady had her skirts in hand and was giving the younger employee a nod of dismissal. "More often the staff than the patients," she grinned in an attempt to introduce a note of levity, before turning away again. "Please, Miss. Dolores is this way."

Dolly was on the basement floor of the Falconwood Asylum, down a long, sterile hall of nude brick. The fire from the gas lamps danced in their wire cages and made the darkness shiver and sporadic. The floor was smooth stone. It was swept and clean but cold, and as Ethel marched to keep in pace with the nurse, the floor clicked its tongue with her every step. It reminded her of the grandfather clock on the second floor of Eden Hall.

"Mrs. Grubb! Can I help you?" There was a man sitting in a small chair before a black, iron, cage door. He was dressed in uniform, and his police cap had been tucked down over his brow to conceal his face in case he dozed. Standing at attention when they'd arrived, the officer blinked, as though unused to doing so, before looking them both over.

"I need inside, please."

"And this is—"

"She's a relative of Mr. and Mrs. Arsenault." Nurse Grubb sighed and stood aside, glancing at Ethel as though for confirmation.

"My name is Ethel Arsenault, but... Is all this really necessary?"

The nurse raised her hands and turned back towards the direction they'd come. "You will have to ask the bailiff. We just run the Nest and see to its chicks. Usually, the cells aren't guarded."

Ethel watched the woman leave like an anxious child abandoning a task. As she turned to the guardsman, the gentleman sighed, and scratched at his head before retrieving the key at his belt.

"Bailiff? I'm sorry, Officer...?"

"Officer Pye." The lock made a noise like a heavy shackle falling open upon the cold, stone floor. "And yes... unfortunately it's all standard protocol. Dolly Arsenault has been arrested and is awaiting trial, so we are required by law to have someone here to guard her." When he turned, it was with a rueful frown meant to take the bite from his words. "She *is* being well cared for, Miss. The ladies here are all very sweet and accommodating."

"Are there others being kept down here?" she asked, watching as the bailiff flung open the door to let her through. Ethel stepped inside, and he closed it behind her.

"There are... but the inmates here are all a part of the Falconwood institution."

Ethel bit her lip and marched down the cellar hall with the officer at her heels. Several thin, square hatches lined the red-bricked walls, while windows hovered above the ground at the top of the outer partition like halos.

"Does she have a window in her room, at least?" Could such a place be a mercy? How much worse was jail than this?

The officer was silent and let the footfalls carry the conversation to its conclusion as they passed a bend. A hatch, positioned alongside the outer wall, was set away from the others, indicating a larger room beyond it. One had to step up into the doorway to enter the cell, and yet the passage leading into the door's nook was short. There were slabs of iron that slid away on the bottom of the hatch, and a few slits at the top, while the panel itself seemed well worn, like a barn door.

"Watch your step up, Miss. If you need anything, I'll be right outside the door." He lifted the bolt that held the hatch shut and motioned for her to continue as he stepped aside. The lock was nothing complicated.

There was no key, nor chain, but a single shaft of iron controlled by the will of its jailor.

Ethel stepped in and groaned from the effort it took to push the door away. On the other side, the room was large, less cold, less bare and less scary. The sight of Dolly turning in cue of Ethel's arrival gave her pause, and for a moment, the two basked in each other's presence like groundhogs emerging for spring.

"Etty!"

"Dolly!" Ethel rushed inside and toppled over the elevated threshold into Dolly's waiting arms. The girl was warm and energetic—like the sunny day that had greeted her when Ethel first arrived at Eden Hall. But she was also kindred— another soul caught up in the turmoil that threatened their idyllic garden hall.

Or was she?

Dolly, did you do it?

"I'm so sorry I haven't visited. The mud, the rain, it's been impossible to get the wagons out." Ethel gave another squeeze, as though to say goodbye to her. As soon as she let go, it could be that the Dolly she so hoped to love as a sister, had been a monster all along.

"Are you all right?" Ethel asked, pulling away and holding the girl at an arm's length as she looked upon her face.

Dolly had aged, though whether it was due to the dour conditions of her keep, or from the woe of her recent loss, Ethel was unsure. Her hair was down, but halfway pinned in ribbon atop her head. Her clothes weren't worn, but plain, and she had stockings, slippers, and a shawl to keep warm. Dolly's room was spacious enough, with small comforts like a rug upon the floor, a quilt on the bed, and a screen in which to dress behind. There was a window as well, small, squat and square, but that faced the direction of the sun from atop the wall. She had a chest of clothes, and a desk in which to write and wash, as well as a cross, above her door and at the foot of her bed.

What things have you said beneath it?

Ethel took a step away and sighed as Dolly moved towards the table. She fetched the chair and proffered it before sitting on the bed.

"Oh Ethel, I'm so sorry for everything! It's so good to see you. I've not stopped thinking about Eden Hall ever since that day. Please—" She lent forward and took Ethel's hand, leading her to sit. "You need to tell me how everyone's doing? Is everyone all right, I—" Dolly hung her head like a dummy whose head had snapped. "I'm so sorry! Tell them how sorry I am? I never wanted any of this to happen!"

"Any of what, Dolly?" Ethel replied, her doubts transformed in the wake of the woman's despair. "You've not done anything wrong. You are a victim in all this! What have you to apologise for?" She reached forward into a wide embrace, and drew Dolly in.

You've done nothing wrong! Nothing!
Please tell me it's nothing...

Dolly cried and stiffened at first, but as her body slumped and Ethel moved to catch her, Dolly's sobbing became an outpour until she heaved in breaths, exhausted. "Maybe I could have helped him? Done something more than I did in the first place?"

"What more could you have done?"

Dolly shook her head and grasped both of Ethel's palms within her own. "I'm so sorry... I loved him so much. Ernie was... he didn't deserve what happened. I should never have waited to call the police, not for a single moment! And if you hadn't been coerced by me to drink so much..."

Ethel released the breath she'd been holding in and leant forwards to reassure her. "It wasn't your fault." *Was it?* "You were only trying to get some sleep, to keep Ernie from worrying about your sleepwalking!"

Was it you who had poisoned the wine?
Why hadn't Bertram suspected?

No... Bertram must know.

Was it that he wished to eliminate all potential suspects as the case narrowed its focus?

This is why you are inside Falconwood, Dolly, and Beulah is not.

Had the constable been bullying her? Attempting to force Ethel into an admission against Beulah's good character? It was likely that the constable suspected Dolly but wanted to erase the potential of another assailant. Else he wanted to gauge the relationship between Ethel and her maid, or Ethel and her maid and Al Carlow.

Ethel had a hard time faulting him for it. Bertram was a man of logic, of profession... and above all else he was in her brother's corner.

Her brother, who was the victim in all this.

"I'm sorry Ethel. I loved Ernie, too! *So* much. I'd do anything to bring him back."

Ethel hugged her, brought back to reality by the wounds in the young girl's eyes.

If neither Dolly nor Beulah poisoned the wine, who was it?

Maybe there was no poison?

No! No. It must have been the burglar.

But it made more sense if it was Dolly. There were less questions involved. Loose ends.

"Dolly, I must tell you. *Everyone* is suspect."

"Not so more than I, Ethel. I'm in here, under constant supervision, and I am no fool." She shook her head. "I know they think I killed him."

"Did you?" She caught Dolly's eyes as soon as they were thrown at her and held them. Not ungently, but with the promise of opportunity if Dolly were to admit her sins now and throw herself at Ethel's feet.

Dolly looked away, just a glance at Ethel's cheek before getting caught again. She closed her eyes, as though from being struck and shook her head.

"No. I *loved* Ernest. I truly did. He was the most amazing man, and... I—I was *so* lucky to be his wife." She sniffed and the pain in her features were tangible. "I didn't kill him, Ethel. I never wanted—never could wish for *anything* of the sort. Even though I am surely responsible for his death."

Ethel cradled Dolly in her arms. It was wild and mad, a notion fit for Falconwood, but Ethel believed her. Dolly loved Ernest, and if she hadn't, then Ethel thought she herself must be mad, because what else could love be, but them?

The two women held each other for a while, and when the sobbing stopped and Dolly sat back to breathe, Ethel sniffed and wiped her face.

"Have the police been here to talk to you?"

"Many times," Dolly said, pulling her hair behind her ears. "They ask the same questions and have me repeat what I saw over and over, as though I've any story but the truth."

"Could you tell me what happened?" She pressed her hand upon Dolly's shoulder. "Perhaps... Perhaps I could help you?"

"Oh Ethel, what could you do? Ernest was an affluent man, and Charlottetown will rally to find him justice." She shook her head. "My only hope... my *sole* hope—is that they find the man who shot my Ernie, so that I may be proven innocent." Her head sank again, "How can I rely on *that?*" she cried.

"They will find him!" Ethel tried to smile. "But it takes time. Right now, they are suspecting *everybody.* Working inside out. If a burglar was a random man, the police need pushing in that direction!" She put a hand on Dolly's shoulder. "Tell me who you saw?"

"I just—I saw a man!" She exhaled, and her whole body deflated with her lungs. "It was dark. They fought. A shot rang out in the night..." She licked her lips and drew them together into a straight line. "I thought I was dreaming. I thought—they said they found no sign of break-in."

"Nor a sign of departure," Ethel said. "And..." The sailors had all left. A burglar would probably never be caught, even if the evidence was found. "I'm sorry, Dolly. It looks glum, but... all of Eden Hall stands behind you."

"Eden," she laughed, "that Hall shall never be my Eden again."

No... The Hall remained for Ernest and it was Ernest who called her Eden. *He had always been worthy of her...*

"Has there been any... news? Any other suspects but me?" Dolly glanced away, before a thought seemed to occur to her. "Have you been staying at the Hall? What about the man? Have you heard anything? A noise within the walls?”

“A noise?” Ethel leant away, a shiver dancing down her spine as Dolly nodded.

“I’ve heard Al’s stories, and Adella Ray, talking about ghosts within the Hall... I know it’s preposterous and,” Dolly looked back and forth, “mad, but...what if I’d heard it? Seen it. Talked to it. Could two young women get away with convincing the entire city that ghosts were real? That God was at fault, and His plan is harsh and cruel but somehow tied to a greater good?”

Ethel frowned, and her heart started skipping.

“You suspect a ghost—”

“Have you heard noises from the walls, Ethel? Strange sounds and things misplaced?”

Ethel nodded, her features frozen into place as her eyes began to burn. The relief she saw on Dolly’s face was like an ember in the hearth.

Warmth from what? From knowing that her sister heard them too?

“Thank God—Thank... Heavens? Who is it I thank?”

“Dolly—”

“Ethel! Ethel, please, if you... if you could only convince the constables that it was a ghost. Al and Adella would surely speak up, and... and you have heard it too!”

Had she? Ethel nodded anyway, and then she shook her head. “Wait... Dolly, you really think—what, why—” Her mind was rending itself asunder. *A logical man like Bertram. What would he say?*

Andrew would say—“Why would a ghost kill Ernest?”

Dolly was shaking her head and the warm glow of the ember shook. “Because someone did! And until they are found, our family will suffer. The staff will suffer and the town will hate us all. The burglar will get nothing but away, and those that loved Ernie will always be suspects.” Dolly looked up. “A ghost can save us, Etty.”

“What if they can find the burglar? What about bringing the killer to justice?

“How likely is that? You know they’ve already gotten away. Ernest had nothing but friends, so how could it be anyone else...” She took a deep breath and let it go like a mother releasing a child. “Ernie always said I was bad at cards, but... the probability of them finding someone is low. They’ll hang *me* long before they find them...”

The old, mad woman’s words tolled in Ethel’s brain, and she winced at the resounding dread that hammered in her ears.

“What do they have to hold you here? Should I know something else? Did you—”

Dolly shook her head, and her face grew pale as she covered her mouth and inhaled. “Your brother was a shipping giant. Mayhap I’m here because someone must be.”

The taut surface of Ethel's cheeks, made so by dried sobs, were wet again from weeping. Why had Dolly given up hope? Why was she not furious that a guilty man may get away?

Is there more to the stories of ghosts in the Hall?

Her mind was a library of questions whose books had all tumbled onto the floor. Stumbling through, Ethel held out her hand and stood when Dolly took it.

"Don't give up hope. I am going to help all I can." Ethel patted Dolly's cheek. As Dolly made to stand, Ethel shook her head for the girl to stay. "Let's leave this sad speaking to another time. I've brought you some stuff, and I've a deck of cards if you'd like a game or two?"

Dolly laughed and nodded her head as she wiped at her cheeks with her shawl. "I can only bet that in which a rich man needs, as it's all that fills my days, I'm afraid..." She smiled, and despite the banks beneath her eyes and the redness of her face, there was genuine glee shining from her features. "A game or two would be lovely, Etty."

Chapter 18

They played for three quarters of an hour before the bailiff rapped on the door. The conversation had been kept light, but despite so, the room was thickened by the prison bars, the heavy door, and its smallness. The presence of ghosts lingered like a foul smell, hearkening Ethel back to the strange instances she had witnessed at Eden Hall. Dolly talking to spirits in the wall, her sleepwalking. *Had she been possessed?*

It was impossible to ignore their surroundings enough to be happy, and yet, both women tried, focusing instead on one another and the mirth that derived from the other's presence.

By the time it had come to leave, the sun was shining in thick orange blankets across the cell room floor.

"I'll come visit you again in a few days," Ethel said, holding her Gladstone in front of her as she stood to head for the door. "In the meantime, make sure you keep motivated and optimistic." She leant in to give the girl a hug.

"You as well, Ethel," Dolly replied, the energy in her words expired. It broke Ethel's heart to hear her so dejected, and yet, Ethel was sure as soon as she crept to the corner of the carriage heading home, she'd also feel downcast.

"Beulah, Fritz, and Al..." Ethel paused on the last name, one foot upon the threshold out towards the hall. "They all send their love."

If there was something telling upon the young girl's features, Ethel never saw it. Instead, she witnessed another sad happiness bloom like a puff of flame at the end of a match.

"Thank you, Etty," Dolly said, her arms across her middle. "Tell them I hope to see them soon."

Ethel nodded and swung away, up over the threshold, and across to the hall. Bailiff Pye was already waiting and shut the door before she had a chance to turn and see the girl again.

"Sorry, Miss. The next guard is due to come in soon anyway, so I'll walk you out."

Ethel watched him lock the door and noted again the ease with which the bolt was latched from the outside. Dolly was behind that door, that lock, and that wall of thick, grey stone. Caged like a bird or a fire up a chimney flue.

What of the other tenets of Falconwood's lower cells? Were they girls like Dolly, who saw ghosts and monsters and other mean things—and if they were, why was Ethel allowed out here while they were imprisoned within?

Ghosts. Spectres. Spirits. I've seen monsters at Eden Hall as well.

If she tried to tell Bertram it was a ghost, would Ethel be here too, whispering to Dolly through walls?

Maybe I should be in one of those rooms...

She'd seen the ghosts, heard the noises, felt the *somethings* in the dark, but the mind was weak to the pain of the heart, and she wondered if she'd only seen them, *heard* them, because it was easier to wonder than think.

No more wondering, Ethel.

She looked around as they gained the first floor. Most of the doors were shut. The corridor was empty, save a few trolleys and chairs. All the residents had been packed back into their rooms, and the nurses were gone. The chill of the hall was piercing, stronger now without the small warmth of gathered bodies. The door outside, framed in glass windows, glowed like an ochre void from the sunset beyond.

If only Roland would come through that door...

Gifts of the mind to heal the heart. Only the gifts had fouled, not met expectations and were reliably depressing.

Ethel shuffled through the door and said goodbye to Bailiff Pye before stepping down the stairs. The air was still, and not a breeze could be seen waving through the trees that lined the yard. Al was on his way, sitting in front of the coach with his back slumped, as though expecting bad news and not eager for it. He didn't say anything as she climbed aboard the carriage, but when their eyes met, there were questions in his gaze that gave her pause.

Did you kill my brother? Seduce my sister and my friend? Are you none of the above?

"She's all right. Comfortable. Though," Ethel glanced at the floor, to her Gladstone bag, "her hope may be faltering..."

"I've never seen Miss Dolly sad, and I've worked for Ernest Arsenault since he moved to Charlottetown." He looked away and scratched at the base of his chin. He looked sullen but was it more so by the fact that there wasn't anything to be done? His fear seemed derived *not* from self-preservation, but from the concern over another. A person to whom he cared.

But what do I know? What if my judgments are wrong? Ethel Arsenault sees ghosts, after all.

Perhaps he did love Dolly, and those affections outweighed his own wellbeing. Or perhaps he was innocent all along, and there was a serpent in Eden Hall.

"Whoever killed Ernest deserves to be hung, and I hope they are so."

Al paled, switched his stance, and tossed his head like a horse avoiding the reins. "Miss Etty, I uh—I've never heard you talk like that."

Nor could Ethel ever recall having done so, but in the moment, she had wanted to witness Al Carlow's reaction and see if it proclaimed his guilt.

"Well... I suppose I should say the same," he said, closing the door and leaning in the window. "Mr. Arsenault was a good man. Whoever done it... well, there ain't a reason for it."

He walked away, and the carriage shook as he sat aboard the driver's seat and lit the lamps in preparation for impending nightfall. She watched his back as they began travelling down the long dirt road that led towards Charlottetown.

Her gaze eventually strayed to the sunset. Its pallet washed the fields in strokes of orange and amber, while the mud continued to harden into terracotta. Ethel took out her journal and turned to the drawing of Al before flipping the page to the other side. She began drawing Dolly, but the coal was soured by her avid thoughts and suspicions. Page after page, she tossed away until she gave up and crumbled in a heap upon her lap.

I need to find a ghost.
I need Roland to walk through the door.
I...

Needed to think, and so breathing in her nose to settle herself, Ethel held her head and concentrated on the shuffle of the carriage wheels.

The crunch of dirt... The clop of the horses hooves...

She picked herself up and closed her book, tucking the coal back inside the tin case from whence it came. Ethel leant against the window and watched the setting sun until the ball of flame became blinding and scoured a gash of darkness behind her eyes.

Chapter 19

She was in a room filled with doors, and yet she could not find her way out.

Ethel had watched as the sun melted away into a star-spangled night sky. The few lights that glimmered along the streets of Charlottetown gave way to a city of safe shadows and quiet manners. Few were out tonight, and so the crickets sang with intent to be heard, like a middle child given the floor.

Beulah was asleep when Ethel arrived. She had been napping upon the chaise in the porch and stirred only when Ethel had shaken her awake. Al was in the barns, unhitching the horses when the two women went inside, and Eden Hall was like a belly fit to consume them.

"Why are you sitting outside? You could catch a cold."

Beulah coughed and wiped at the circles beneath her eyes. "I wanted to wait for you."

You were afraid.

Ethel led the poor woman upstairs, squeezing her shoulders and lending support as they went up to Ethel's bedroom. Beulah was afraid of ghosts, of the thing she had seen in the dark, and Ethel couldn't blame her. It was a relief, of sorts, to know that someone like Beulah could believe in ghosts, and yet even so, Ethel shook her head. She needed some time to think. Despite the day she had, Ethel kissed Beulah's brow and tucked her into bed, and then she closed the bed curtain in her room and wandered to her desk.

Suspects: Al Carlow, Dolly Arsenault, Beulah Murphy.

Ethel gazed at the paper on her desk, and the ink that was drying upon it. She scratched out Beulah's name but then rewrote it again.

Motive? Possible affair.

Evidence.

She could hear Beulah snoring already and mumbling something in her sleep. Ethel crossed out her name.

Evidence? Gunshot wound. Bullet removed. Missing—Gun.

No forced entry. Killed on the second floor.

Why is the gun missing?

Ethel underlined the last sentence, and then did so again.

Why is the gun missing?

What *had* happened to the gun? The constable had said that the bullet retrieved from Ernest's wound had matched a revolver that was missing from the cabinet.

But then why did a burglar not bring his own weapon?

It was true that Ernest had inherited a vast collection passed down from his father and great-grandfather, but as much as he was apt to polish and care for his guns, Ernest hardly ever had them loaded.

So why would someone have taken a gun on a whim, and why would it have been loaded?

Did Ernest hear a kerfuffle upstairs and take the gun? If so... where did it go?

Ethel sat up and walked to her bedroom door. Already asleep and snoring, Ethel spared a glance at Beulah before she left the room and vowed to be back post haste.

The house lights were still aglow, though they were only lit in the main chambers and on the stairs. Ernest's study was dark, as it had remained so for days, though the light from the foyer cast its sunny veil to shimmer upon the outline of the room's contents.

If the culprit was Dolly, then why? For money? Ernest wasn't frugal with her, and their marital chambers proves that. Now, as it was, if Dolly was never set free, Ethel would inherit his estate, and the thought of that made her shiver.

What would I even do?

She went to the cabinet and paused. *Who would I have to ask?*

The guns were lined in rows behind a shining panel of glass. At the foot, there was another display box that had been built onto the structure's main frame. Inside, laying upon a carpet of forest green, were several small pistols, displayed to show the barrel of the gun, and its handle.

Ethel recalled the delicate details and polish of the silver-clad revolvers, the satin glow of the red brass flintlocks and steel pistols. They had been a source of pride for her father, whose family tree was rooted in a history of weapon and arms dealing. They would have meant nothing to her if not for the memories of her father. But even so, glancing up towards the rifles that stood like soldiers behind a slab of glass, Ethel noticed a handgun missing. It had been the *Colt Cowboy Gun,* as Ernie had dubbed it. Ivory handle, dark, polished steel with roses running down the barrel. *It was a gun a cowboy'd use,* young Ernie had said. *To keep the bad guys in line!*

It was flashy, and modern—

And missing.

Ethel sighed. *A ghost wouldn't need a gun,* she thought.

It sent a shiver down her spine and caused her skin to prickle. Though the lights were still on in the main foyer, there was a flicker behind her, and she turned, fear spreading panic to her limbs until she backed away towards the cabinet and called out.

"H-hello?" Her voice was soft and meek, and sabotaged an unequivocal reply. Perhaps it was Beulah, or Al? Or Adella? Ethel hadn't seen the girl for days...

There was no reply. Silence filled the space around her like a glaze of hot pitch. Her heartbeat rang in her ears and was the only sound she heard until something thudded away.

THUMP! *THUMp!* *THUmp!THump!Thump!thum-thum-thum-thum-p!*

Ethel sprang around, catching at the latch of the gun cabinet before throwing open the doors. The glass rattled in the wooden frame, but as she pulled a rifle free and aimed it at the foyer, the silence had returned.

Ethel trembled, finding little solace in staring down the length of the firearm. She had cocked the gun to chamber a bullet, hoping that if someone were out there, they would heed and beware. Her father had never abided a loaded gun—not outside of wartime. Ernie followed suit, if only out of respect, but the sound was threatening enough, and surely, whoever was there, didn't know that the gun was empty.

She left the den, the butt of the rifle held up snug against her shoulder. The end of the barrel shook, but as Ethel's eyes scanned the foyer, she saw nothing but the large front door, the dining room across the hall, and the steps towards the upper landing.

I have to turn off the gas, but... Had it been her imagination? Without the light to push it back, would the darkness attack her? She could call for help, for Beulah, but the poor woman was scared enough of phantoms.

Ethel lowered the gun but kept it at her side as she wandered over to twist the valve. She took in a breath and held it, refusing to baulk at the stygian tide that overcame her vision. She wanted to sprint up the stairs, or better yet, wake up to her room and to Beulah snoring away beside her. Instead, she faced the dark, and like the sea, it was suffocating.

Roland, please, if you're there, guide me.

What if he's there but he's angry, Ethel?

She held the railing and her skirts with the gun beneath her arm.

Who killed Ernest Arsenault? Was it Al? Beulah? Dolly?

The stairs creaked and groaned. On the second floor, the grandfather clock began to chime. Ethel paused and looked downstairs like a drowning woman measuring her depth and time. She saw shadows in the dark, winding along the floor in lithe circles like a kraken's limbs. The moon shone down through the windows, blinking from behind a veil clustered with clouds and whispering trees.

The clock struck again… and again and again, and yet she continued in sync of its harmonious chime as it roared hollow throughout Eden Hall.

Who killed Ernie, Etty? Was it Al? Was it Beulah, or Dolly?

I've heard the noise within the walls...
What if the Devil killed Ernie?

She gained the second floor, her chest heaving not from the climb but by the thoughts that were clamouring in her mind. The gun was heavy and weighed down her steps. She wanted to be in her room. Safe. But was it safe? If not for Beulah, Ethel wouldn't have thought so.

The sole lantern that was lit upstairs, glimmered like a light in a marble. The green wallpaper, only just lit by the infant flame, was illuminated at its core, and lit up like a lime. It was situated halfway down the hall, between her room and Beulah's vacant quarters. The brass knob that controlled the flow of gas was polished like a new coin, and as Ethel slipped along the floor in her stocking feet, she gasped when the light went out.

She had been staring right at it, and it was like a scar across her vision. Ethel stopped and held up the gun, turning to watch the stairs as she held her breath. The walls were nothing but tar, the portraits and mirrors voids of black water. But in the murk and mire of the second floor, Ethel saw a body in the darkness.

"Don't move!"

It stepped out from the door to the upper landing, its form nothing but a pitched-soaked blur that slipped along the floor like a ribbon of grease. Ethel backed away, poised on the balls of her feet like a hare who would outrun the wolf. Her teeth were chattering, and her eyes watered as it continued to move like a serpent upon the water.

Was this the thing that killed Ernie? Was this the—

She saw Roland in the darkness. His square chin, beard, and moustache. He was wearing a long coat, with his collar undone, but his hair was longer and unkempt.

It was Roland!

Roland...

Roland had come through the door!

Ethel wept, the weight of the gun becoming too much as she stared at the man in front of her.

"Roland... is it you? Have you come?"

He stopped, and the dark began to shift as his features emerged in gradient ebony. "I didn't mean to do it, Ethel. I didn't..."

She refused to blink for fear of him vanishing, but as her eyes watered and his form became blurry, a fierce despair poured out from her mouth. "Roland... *What* did you do?"

You boarded the boat. You died at sea. You left me alone without even a last name to remember you.

You came back...

...and murdered my brother.

He was a sable vacuum, and though his face and form were outlined in a line of white, as he drew forward, Ethel held up the unloaded gun.

"Ethel, I'm coming to you."

Her muscles spasmed as her finger hovered over the trigger. Though the gun was empty, she was unable to touch it. *Never point a gun at someone unless you mean to shoot them.*

Her father's words. They ran circuits in her head. The implication of raising a gun meant she may be tested to use it, and she was. His movements were measured, but he drew forward like a lion stalking its prey. Ethel winced, her heart breaking in two. "Don't come any closer!" she hollered. "Why did you kill him? What had Ernest ever done to earn your wrath?"

He didn't answer but, with a jolt, sprang forward like a bolt of lightning. The darkness that was his form yawned as he neared, and the rifle was like a spear he was trying to avoid. He darted left to break her aim, but Ethel's finger pulled the trigger as he tried to get within reach.

The gun roared thunder. The light from the blast illuminated the room for the single second it took to see the blood fly through the air. A guttural thud from the man falling shook the portraits on the wall and shattered the glass of the grandfather clock as he fell against it.

Ethel lurched back against Beulah's bedroom door. The force of the gun blast was like a push from a strapping young man, and she grasped her shoulder where the buttstock had sat.

Her vision was gone, the faint lines obliterated by the sudden spark of light. Ethel fumbled in the dark, hearing the rapid breaths of a foe fallen. "Oh God," she gasped, dropping the gun as its weight became an anchor.

What have I done?

"Are y-you…. all right?"

There were coughs and sputtering, clinks of glass, but as she tried to focus her eyes, Ethel reeled back. A hand in her hair shoved her sideways, and as she fell into the wall, ornaments crashed and broke on the floor.

"Where's the gun?" he blurted with his breath hot on her face. He smelled of gin and limes.

Ethel squirmed, her heart a mad badger in her chest. He was larger than her but slumped and relied on the wall for balance. As the warmth of blood splattered on her cheek, Ethel moved, running towards the stairs as he fell, and his body made a slapping sound against the carpet.

The hall was a blur, and as if she were in the belly of a giant at the bottom of the sea, the darkness disoriented her. Glass shards stuck in her feet, but as Ethel sprinted to the stairs, hobbling on bloody stockings, something grabbed at her skirts. She lurched, her eyes wide as white medallions, and her heartbeat pounded against her heaving chest. Though the grip was weak, the weight of the man threw her off balance, and stumbling to right herself, Ethel screamed as her legs tangled in her dress and sent her over the bannister of the upper floor landing.

There was the sound of somebody calling her name, and the screams that poured from her own mouth. Both were dwarfed by the words that bore welts on her brain.

Why are you killing us, Roland?

Why did you kill my brother? Why did you shoot him!

The pain of the unforgiving floor devoured her.

In the distance, she heard a voice. "You shot him, Ethel. *You.*"

I... killed...

Me?

Chapter 20

Mud and dirt. Together they were almost impossible to dig out of. But set the Fundy Bay on top, and one could be entombed forever.

Ethel's body sunk beneath the mud until her limbs were bound and her legs were unmoving. Though she was pressed down like linen beneath a flat iron, her body was hollow, and her mind was a prisoner within it.

Quick photographs fluttered behind her eyes like playing cards released to the floor. Her heartbeat in her arm and her hip, and another pounded between her ears. It was all she could focus on, and she realised that it was not a heartbeat, but the drums of pain and ache beating her to consciousness.

She heard a voice from far away.

"Ethel! Ethel, are you awake?"

Was she? The voice was distorted, like it had been said from inside a glass jar. Ethel was unsure to whom the voice belonged, but neither could she tell if her eyes were open or where she was.

"Is..." her own voice was a stranger, said at the pit of the very same glass jar.

"Miss Beulah! Ethel is waking. Please, can you alert the doctor?"

Her head was a swollen pumpkin ready to pop, but as Ethel tried to focus and sit herself up, a knife in her arm caused her to scream.

"I haven't got the plaster on yet, so don't let her wave her arm about!"

A reassuring hand pressed upon the base of her back and helped to set her down on the bed. The scent of dust was accompanied by the sight of Constable Bertram. He was wearing a suit, one she hadn't seen before. The brass on his double-breasted waistcoat winked as he removed his hand and examined her face.

Beulah was calling her name from another room, and Ethel realised she was in her quarters at Eden Hall. The curtains on the four post bed were tied, and the fire had been stoked. Mr. Bertram was in the room, sitting on a chair next to the bed. Next to him was another man, who looked to be a doctor by his very fine Gladstone bag.

"Miss Ethel!" Beulah called. The plump young woman entered through the bedroom door, and Ethel blinked to ensure her vision had restored. Her body was aching, disturbing her senses.

How did I get here?

What is happening?

"Can you give her something for the pain, Doctor Johnson?"

The other man shook his head as he set out the tools to begin. Bandages, plaster, scissors, and a few amber glass bottles. "Ether could dull the pain, but it's also a sedative. She needs to stay awake. It would be wise for someone to stay with her for a few hours to keep her from falling asleep."

"Is she going to be all right?"

The doctor nodded, and he looked up towards Miss Murphy as she stood across the bed and exhaled her relief. "Do you know how to bandage, Miss?"

"I do."

The doctor nodded and snapped the mouth of his Gladstone shut. "Good. The materials are all there. I've included a few painkillers for after. They'll cause her to sleep, so don't give her any before evening." He was already walking towards the door, as though anything else was common knowledge.

"Is it only her arm that I should bandage?"

The doctor was at the threshold when Ethel noticed a few other men loitering in the hallway.

"Yes. Everything else will heal without bandages, but she ought to get plenty of rest."

"Doctor," Bertram said, turning towards the door, as though throwing a rope in hopes of corralling him.

"You may visit my office for the medical report later, Constable. I'll have it set aside as soon as I prepare it." The doctor inclined his head, privy to Ethel's concerning stare. "See to your witness, Constable. Excuse me."

He left, closing the door behind him and muting the commotion that was going on outside of it.

"I'll start preparing the plaster," Beulah said, nodding as she bent to retrieve the materials set out on the opposite side of the bed.

Mr. Bertram was in front of the door, rubbing his eyes. His suit, though new, was wrinkled, and his hair was tousled and unkempt. Accompanying the smell of dust was the scent of sweat and pipe smoke.

"What time is it?" A tune was playing in her head, and as the notes meandered across her mind, Ethel recalled the words and refrain of the night's chorus.

"It's early. The sun hasn't risen y—"

"Wait." Her eyes wandered the maze she was scrambling through her in mind. The strength of the song pulled her towards the exit, and yet as she arrived, Ethel blanched.

"Roland... What of the man I killed? Did I kill him? I didn't—"

"He's fine, Ethel," Bertram said, turning towards the bed and taking a seat at the chair. "Well... not *fine,* but he'll live. You shot him, Ethel."

Her heart was rooting in her chest, entangling itself around her vitals. *Was it Roland? Did I see* him? It was as though she were being contorted in every direction. The implication of every outcome was as bad as the last.

Her mind was throbbing, more so by her inability to think. "Please, Andrew," she said, pulling her unpinned hair away from her eyes with her unbroken arm. "Can you tell me what happened? Who was it I saw? I... my mind is in shambles."

Bertram smiled, though it was sad. Ethel had seen those smiles before. They were poorly concealed frowns harbouring a Trojan horse filled with pity. Her dread was building, ready to burst, and Ethel held her breath.

Andrew replied, "You've just woken up, Ethel. You fell from the second story landing. The man you shot—"

A man! Not a ghost... not Roland.

Unless...

"His name is Johnathan Dowie. We don't know a lot, yet, but we believe he has been living at Eden Hall. He's a sailor."

A sailor? The burglar?

"L-living?" she blurted as her mind caught up.

Andrew lost his smile, and the line that was his mouth was straight and stoic. "We found evidence in the attic. Your brother's gun, missing a few bullets, as well as some personal effects." He looked up to Miss Murphy, who had prepared the plaster and was waiting.

Ethel looked sidelong, then back towards the constable before unbuttoning her blouse. "You can go ahead, Beulah. I'm not bashful of the constable."

The comment made the young man's face turn red.

Ethel pretended not to notice as Beulah began to see to her arm.

"Mr. Dowie has been taken in for questioning… but there is evidence of him hiding in several small spaces between the walls. Trash and whatnot, but also evidence of loitering."

"He was living in the *walls?*" Ethel looked askance at the several portraits hanging upon her bedroom walls as though they'd been privy to this secret information. "Why?"

"I've a theory," Bertram replied, reluctant to answer, "But I wish to question him first, and I wanted to see that you were all right before I left for the station."

"Mr. Bertram was worried for you, Miss Ethel."

He was trying not to look at her in her current state of undress, and Ethel couldn't help but smile at his propriety. The plaster was cool, and she winced as Miss Murphy went about making the cast.

Ethel's head was a trainwreck, filled with soot and ashes that obscured the extent of the damage. A burglar had been living in Eden Hall, and he'd been captured. *That means Dolly has been telling the truth, and she'll be set free, right?*

Ethel laid her head back. She wanted to sleep. "Is Eden Hall safe?" she asked.

"It's secure," Bertram replied with a nod. "We checked every nook and cranny, Miss Ethel. You are safe here, which is why you yet remain."

"And Aloysius?"

The constable pursed his lips and looked over his shoulder towards the door. With a glance to Miss Murphy, he leant in as though to whisper, though his voice came out loud and matter of fact. "There were no fingerprints belonging to Mr. Carlow anywhere upstairs."

Ethel smiled. *Which means he didn't do it, and in the future, if rumours are spread, Miss Murphy can know from the constable's own mouth that Al was declared innocent.*

"I'm sorry to ask," Ethel replied, aware that he had held her in confidence.

Mr. Bertram frowned but nodded with a small snort as Ethel glanced back to squeeze at Beulah's hand.

"And can you tell me any more about Mr. Dowie?" She wondered if she'd ever forget that name. "Why was he here? What was his motive for... for hurting Ernest?" *Was he a disgruntled employee? Someone displaced?*

"He is being seen at Doctor Johnson's private practice. Once his injuries are assessed and seen to, we will question him."

"He is going to live?"

"Yes."

She sighed, feeling something lift from off her shoulders. "Thank you, Andrew."

He tipped his chin to glance at Miss Murphy. "I'll be back as soon as I find out more." He then donned a cap that had been resting on the side of the chair.

Ethel watched him go, his back blurring as tears poured out from the inner corners of her eyes.

"Miss Ethel, am I hurting you?"

Ethel shook her head. "No, Beulah. I'm sorry. I just... feel relieved." She wiped at the sides of her nose and rubbed at her eyes to clear her vision. *A man in the house. Not a ghost.* Not her Beloved, come from the sea to spread woe and misery. *I'll try to make you a happy memory, Roland, and not a phantom in a grave I've lain upon.*

Her sister would be home soon. Beulah and Al would no longer be suspects in her brother's murder. "I want to sleep. I think I could finally do so comfortably."

Each day was a step towards recovery. Towards it not hurting so much anymore. Though Beulah chuckled, her relief was not as apparent as Ethel's when she spoke, "You heard the Doctor. You won't be doing any of that for a few hours, and with this arm..." Beulah held up the bandages. "I'm not sure of *comfort.*"

Ethel's mood wavered, and looking up at her, she noticed how much paler Beulah looked now than when they had journeyed together from Summerside. Paler and a bit older, though she wore a flowered comb in her hair now.

"Beulah, did you see him?" she asked, just now considering the sight Miss Murphy would have been witness to after the roar of the rifle went off.

The woman looked down and concentrated on laying the plaster and bandages. "I didn't recognize him. He looked young and scared, but he was bleeding to death." Beulah was quiet, but before the silence fouled, she looked up with tears in her eyes. "I was so scared for you Miss Ethel," she continued, leaning across the bed as Ethel moved to hold her against her chest. Her hip was paining, but the comfort she found within Miss Murphy was worth more than the ache of her fall.

A noise from outside the room caused the two women to look up, and a man's voice from the other side of the door shouted their leave as footsteps clamoured down the main front stairs.

The officers were all leaving.

"I suppose I have a mess to clean," Beulah said, resuming her task as she wiped at her eyes.

Ethel waved her good hand, then winced from pain. "After this, why don't you read to me from my book."

Beulah laughed, with more sincerity this time. "*I'd* fall asleep if I read one of your books, Miss Ethel."

"Well then, just turn the page, will you? I'll read as you take care of me."

"Fine, fine..." Beulah dismissed. "Just don't do the voices. I need a steady hand you know."

Ethel agreed. "You wouldn't fetch the book for me, would you?" Her vision was still blurry, and she wondered if she could read the words. As expected, Beulah huffed, and the kerfuffle of her friend made Ethel giggle. "Don't lose my page, please. I think I'm on chapter thirty-six."

"You're going to read to me from the last chapter of the ding dong book?"

"It's not the last," Ethel insisted, letting her head sway against her pillows. "Nobody's gotten married yet."

Chapter 21

As the week went on to digest each day, Ethel found a queer sort of calm in the routine of Eden Hall. Ernest's funeral had to be prepared as the thaw reached farther into the frozen topsoil, and the house, once again, had to be cleaned from the passage of mindless police officers. Print powder and mud, and the leftover glass and chinaware found in the nooks upstairs, all had to be brought down and assessed.

Most of the blood had been picked up from the floor, but not all had been scrubbed away. Splatter was found all the way down the hall towards Beulah's room, and on the chandelier that hung from the second floor landing. It was hard to believe they were cleaning up blood, but as Ethel scrubbed at the macabre stains, she had to wonder if any of it had been her brothers.

Due to his work, Constable Bertram had been unable to visit since the arrest. The papers were happy to oblige each week with a suitable update rife with conjecture and rumour.

"The same papers that were fast to condemn Miss Dolly this time last week, are now raising Hell about her not being let free!" Al sat back in one of the old wooden chairs that were tucked against the kitchen countertop. A straw hat was hitched up on the top of his head, and his boots were kicked together across the polished wooden floor. Beulah was puttering around making breakfast but made sure to shoot him a glare every time she managed to avoid tripping over his shoes. He was reading from the Summerside Journal.

"Apparently, Mr. John Dowie is now at the Pownal Square Jail. So, I guess that means they must've got all that lead outta him."

Beulah kicked his foot, ushering Mr. Carlow to move as she wandered past him towards the stove. Ethel was at the table, writing out cheques and signing papers regarding her brother's funeral.

"Watch what you say around Miss Ethel!" Beulah chided, rolling up her sleeves as she grabbed the bread pans and began to grease them.

Al shrugged but continued reading on his own. "Around here, we call it Harvie's Brig," he muttered.

"Isn't that jail infamous for public hangings?" Ethel looked up, catching Al's eye before the man risked a glance towards Beulah.

"Well... I suppose it is, yes." He tipped his hat to scratch at the base of his hairline. "But I wouldn't be worrying too much about that, Miss Ethel."

"I read in the Examiner that there's been a lot of opposition to the death penalty, especially in and amongst Charlottetown. I wonder if they'll hang him."

Ethel signed another document without hardly reading it. *I hope Dolly will be back soon. I hate to even think it, but I've had my fill of funerals...*

"Do you think Dolly will be sending word soon?" Ethel asked, picking her head up from the table.

Al looked relieved. "Well, I've got the coach all ready!" he said, rolling up the newspaper. "So as soon as she does, we'll be on our way."

"I can hardly wait..."

Ethel rubbed her eyes and watched as Al stood up from the chair. They had all just finished breakfast together, and Fritz was set to return to the house. Doctor Johnston had been around to check on Ethel several times, and it had been at his discretion that Fritz Humphrey was to return to Eden Hall for rest and the reinstating of light duties.

Ethel was happy about it. She was also sure that Fritz would be relieved, as Al often reported that Fritz only opened his mouth to eat, and to grouch at how bored he was, staying at his sister's house.

It had been a week since John Dowie had climbed down from the third floor, and yet Ethel's spirits were slowly climbing. Her brother's killer had been caught, Eden Hall was safe once more, and its Lady was set to return any day. The terrible chasm Ethel had fallen into when her brother had been slain, was rising beneath her with every spark of joy she managed to light beneath her heel, and now knowing that Beulah and Al were innocent, Ethel's hope was ignited.

She found out right away that John Dowie had lived, and though the feelings were strange to process, Ethel was glad she had not ended his life. Doctor Johnston told her that he'd survived only due to the rifle's close range that had reduced the spread of the ballistics and because Dowie had been facing straight on when the gun went off. Ethel hoped to meet him someday, to see the man who murdered her brother. She figured she'd go with Dolly...

* * *

"Ethel? Constable Bertram is here to see you."

Ethel looked up from her brother's desk. It was evening time, and the candles shone like flickering wisps from off the mantlepiece. The light from the foyer lit the outline of the large, mahogany desk in the middle of the room. The gaslit lanterns on the walls were in shadows.

"Are you here signing papers in the dark?" Beulah huffed, looking across the room before crossing it to light the sconce.

"You'll be a blind old shrew if you read without light! I'm terribly sorry, Constable, I'd no idea my Ethel was a bat."

With the favour of darkness, the officer hid a chuckle.

Ethel set down her pen. "I was working, and it got dark. I had figured I'd finish before then." Her frown deepened as the light came on.

Beulah turned to receive it. "Look at your eyes narrowing! You're like an *abhartach*, allergic to light."

As though to press the sentiment home, Ethel was wearing a black tea gown with a slight train. It hung as a coat around her shoulders. She had not been out at all today, and so her hair was done up in a simple chignon that was letting go at the sides. Ethel stood as the light made a strong popping sound.

"Mr. Bertram," she called, standing from her brother's chair to cross the room. He was wearing a long coat, dappled with rain upon the shoulders.

"Miss Ethel." He nodded his head, inhaling as though to resituate himself.

Ethel's brows drew together as he received her greeting and paused. "Do you have Dolly with you?" she asked, having expected him to say so right away. She looked past him, wondering if she had been made the target of a jest. "Has Dolly been discharged?"

He didn't answer right away, and the pause was enough to sink her stomach.

Ethel wrung her hands and looked back inside her brother's office. With only a brief gesture from Mr. Bertram, she stepped back to sit upon an armchair in the corner. The constable followed, picking up the desk chair before taking a seat in front of her.

"Ethel…" Mr. Bertram took her hand before pausing, as though to reconsider the act. Looking down, he swallowed hard, and placed his other hand atop her own and squeezed.

"Dolly isn't coming home. She has been placed in quarantine."

Ethel's heart leapt against her chest, and she sat forward. "For what?"

"They believe it could be Typhus."

"Typhus!"

Mr. Bertram shook his head, his piercing eyes intent on holding her where he could not. His grip upon her hand tightened. "They don't know everything yet. She's been ill a few days, and it has popped up at Falconwood before, so… the nurses are taking extra precautions."

Ethel sighed and caught her head as it threatened to roll from off her shoulders.

"That's not all, I'm afraid."

"Andrew, I'm not certain I can take anymore." She rubbed at her temples and pressed the pad of each thumb onto the back of her eyelid until she was unable to see when she opened her eyes.

"I'm sorry, Ethel. I wanted to tell you in person before..."

"Before?" She sensed his hesitation, sourced by their growing fondness of one another. Ethel could tell it bothered him. His inability or *reluctance* to dutifully relay the information to her for concern of the pain it'd cause. Ethel didn't like the thought of forcing that position on him, and so despite her trepidation, she carried on.

Fall down all the way before getting yourself back up, Ethel.

Andrew exhaled with a sigh and sat up straight, like an old oak ready to catch the rain.

"Dolly has admitted that John Dowie, a sailor from north of the Island, was her lover." He gripped her by the shoulders, as though expecting her to fall forward. "Dolly has admitted... to having an affair."

Chapter 22

Her belly was a warlock's stew and gargled from the toxic ingredients Andrew Bertram chopped and threw inside. Ethel was confused, like a child with a block of wood who was trying to shove it through the cylindrical hole.

"How—Dolly *admitted?*"

Surely the constable isn't wrong? Ethel trusted him. Andrew Bertram was a lawful man... but Dolly was her sister, and Dolly had *loved* Ernest. How could that all be true when the words he spoke were surely not?

Andrew nodded, and again her hands were in his own. "We spoke to Dolly after Mr. Dowie was brought in to be treated—"

"When she was sick?"

Again, he nodded. "We took all precautions, but after speaking with her, Dolly admitted that she was having an affair with Mr. Dowie."

Ethel shook her head. "Why would she—"

"We believe she is trying to save him by pinning the blame upon herself. *I* believe she thinks the man won't hang if the community is irate with *her.*

"What does this Mr. Dowie say?"

"At first, he said he was a cat burglar, trying to rob the house. But then... he later admitted to staying in the house at Mrs. Arsenault's request. He also admitted to... to shooting your brother, Ethel."

Ethel's nostrils flared, and from the base of her head a spark of pain ignited that exploded behind her eyes. She was holding everything in, like an ill-suited mason jar that had become unsealed. With a gasp, and another quick intake of air, she slumped forward, and held her mouth as though afraid her soul would flee.

"How—" she turned away and got up from the armchair to regard the desk. Ernest's papers were on the top. Arrangements for his funeral, invitations, a note from the tailor for Dolly's funeral wear...

"Ethel," he reached for her hand as it fell from his, and she snapped it away as he implored her to sit.

"You... you pitted them against each other, didn't you?"

"What? Ethel, I—"

"If Dolly changed her story—if she said she did it—it's because she thought John Dowie would hang." *Because she loves him?* "And if Dowie first admitted to being a burglar... if he collaborated her story... that means he must have changed his mind after finding out about Dolly's confession. Which means you *told* him she confessed as leverage!" *Because they love each other...*

Andrew stood, and instead of mirroring her ire, he was stiff, with his mouth just slightly agape. "Miss Ethel, I don't understand. If Dolly was having an affair with a man who killed your brother—"

"I should want to know? I should not be here making excuses for them? Naming you as the villain?" she hollered, flinging her arms out before wrapping them around her middle. Her legs were giving out, unable to hold herself steady from the beating of her heart.

I should want to know, but I don't! I don't want to hear it from you, Andrew. I don't want to hear it from anybody but Dolly.

She said we were sisters...

"She said she loved him..." Ethel sobbed, sinking to the floor before Andrew could catch her. He stooped to one knee and braced her shoulders once again.

"Ethel, please... speak to me."

She shook her head and tucked her chin against her chest in a vain attempt to keep everything in. Ethel had shattered, and yet here she was clutching at her broken pieces in an attempt to reclaim her shape.

"I haven't even known Dolly for very long," she said, rocking herself back and forth. "But since Roland died I... It's like I've been clawing for something—anything, to get me out of this casket of mad despair! Ernest and Dolly..." Ethel opened her eyes, recalled the first day she'd arrived at Eden

Hall, all the conversations she had had with Ernie and Dolly, "after so much mourning and self-loathing they—they gave me hope."

His eyes were shining as she looked at him. They spoke volumes when his mouth could not. Looking down at his chest, Ethel leant in, and closed her eyes as his arms enveloped her. His heart beneath his dusty suit beat in rhythmic pulse, and yet as she listened, her own began to match his rhythm.

"What is going to happen to them, Andrew?"

He was breathing close to her ear, and she heard the hitch in his inhale as he started to respond, "There is going to be a trial. Most likely Dolly will be released, but John Dowie will be hung if he is found guilty." He paused, and she could tell he was deliberating whether he should tell her all the information. He continued, though a large part of Ethel wished he hadn't. "Mr. Dowie has admitted to killing your brother, and Ernest was an affluent man. Charlottetown won't let him live."

"And I should be happy about that," Ethel mused. "Right?"

Andrew didn't reply, but as his arms tightened around her, Ethel thought it must be in consequence of her fleeting character.

How small I am.

If Andrew had pitted the lovers against each other, then that means there was affection between them. Dolly wanted to share the blame, and Dowie was taking it all for himself. It crushed Ethel's heart because they both were willing to die for the other, but Ernest had died for them both.

"I want to talk to him. I want to see John Dowie."

Andrew pulled away and looked her in the eyes as though to see if she'd gone mad. "Why?"

"I want to see the man who killed my brother. I want to meet him." *I want to see who Dolly betrayed my brother for.* "And then I want to talk to Dolly."

"Ethel—"

She looked up at him, and unwinding, Ethel reached towards his face and pressed a palm to his cheek. He needed a shave. The distinct, yet masculine texture of his beard rubbed like tree bark beneath her fingertips.

I wonder what it'd feel like to have a man's beard cross your face for the first time.

She leant forward and kissed him, her lips unsure and untrained as he softened from stiff, unyielding stone to the clay that first made man. The pliant slope of his lips gave way, and she received the warmth of his mouth until his beard caressed her cheeks.

Serrated yet shallow, like a rake within the garden.

Chapter 23

Ethel had tried to see Dolly before Ernest's funeral. Everyday, she had instructed Al to prepare the stagecoach, and on occasion he did, despite it being a fruitless endeavour. Falconwood Asylum was closed off, quarantined until it was determined no cases of Typhus were present. Ethel had stood in front of Falconwood and begged to be let inside, but despite her fervour and mad determination, Al had come to fetch her, and talk sense until she agreed to leave.

"Miss Ethel, you need to stop—"

"I can't Beulah. Not until I know for sure." She was madder now than when she was seeing Roland in the hall. When Ernest's funeral came upon them, Ethel wept until her body bowed and her heart slopped out upon the open gravesite.

Andrew was there to support her, as was Beulah and Al, Fritz, and Adella. Many people of Charlottetown had attended, but of course, as Ethel stood to do the eulogy, the one person she wished to see was of course, not there.

"I feel so bad for poor Ethel. Dolores was having an affair even after she'd arrived at Eden Hall!"

"If you ask me, the harlot should hang alongside that Dowie lad. Imagine hiding your lover in the very house your husband had built for you."

"Miss Arsenault has lost so much, poor dear."

"Perhaps she is bad luck."

Perhaps she was. But despite the rumours and condolences, Ethel stood at the height of the tide of mourners and received their comfort without knowing most. It was impossible to not feel the hole that Dolly's absence had created, even if everyone seemed willing to fill it with their gossip.

For the first time since Ethel had arrived, Eden Hall was bursting with people. The wake was in the parlour, and the bay windows that opened into the yard were ajar to let in the scent of flowers and the sea. By the time it all had ended, Ethel went up to bed, feeling like she was dragging the body of her brother with her.

"Is there anything else I can do, Miss Ethel?"

"No, thank you, girls."

Beulah was at the foot of the stairs, her plump cheeks red and chapped from the events of the day. Adella was stacking the chairs. Both women had insisted that Ethel go to bed whilst they cleaned. Bertram had left minutes ago, but Ethel had no energy to even lift her head.

"Miss Ethel?" Beulah called, causing her to pause. Her palm stuck to the bannister despite her body's inclination to continue on before it could give out. "The constable—Mr. Bertram said... that as soon as you felt up to it, he'd take you to see... well..." Beulah looked aside, predicting her interest as Ethel turned upon the stairs.

"Tell Andrew to come tomorrow."

Beulah looked taken aback. "Miss Ethel, are you sure?"

I'm not. "No. But why wait? I'll be ready in the morning."

Ethel continued up the stairs, ignoring Beulah as she turned to bid Adella to chase after the constable before he could leave in his stagecoach. The upper landing had been cleaned and polished, and in some cases, the paint had been touched up to hide the hint of stains. But as Ethel halfway crawled across the final stair, she saw on the base of the bannister, between the rungs, a dollop of black blood that had formed a crust against the wood.

Is this preferable to blind hope?

Her stomach was hurting, and so Ethel continued, crawling up to the landing until she saw the bedroom doors all ajar.

She crawled into bed until Beulah called her name the next morning.

Chapter 24

Harvey's Brig was an iron safe of a building. Its four outer walls were sturdy and tall, supported by unpainted, wooden siding. The structure was topped with a pitched gabled roofline, and a chimney that was twice as thick as any of the windows. Though there were several on the face of the building, their scarcity was felt on its flanks, which were only visible above the twelve-foot, white, wooden fence that encompassed every side of the jail but its front.

Alders, thistles and crabgrass grew alongside the fence and the road, but the area was devoid of much else. The crunch of gravel was a precursor to the stagecoach door swinging open. Ethel was sitting inside, her black skirt arranged to one side as Andrew Bertram held out a hand for her.

He had accompanied Ethel from Eden Hall, but the two had said very little to one another besides the normal day pleasantries. The idle small talk was brittle and lacking in the face of what was to come. Ethel saw the hesitation in Andrew's eyes, the silent petition for her to return home. But Falconwood was still under quarantine, and Ethel determined that if she was barred from seeing Dolly, she'd hear what her lover had to say instead.

The jailor, Thomas Harvey, met them at the door in a waistcoat and trousers. The day was clammy, though with the promise of sun later on. The morning clouds had begun to thaw and were departing a stone-grey sky.

Ethel thanked the constable as he escorted her out from the stagecoach, and then turned her attention to the jailor. He was a stout man, well-built but short. He had a moustache that wrapped around his face towards his ears and a severe brow that was emphasised by his receding hairline.

Thomas Harvey greeted Andrew first before his gaze swung towards Ethel. He cleared his throat, which jiggled a small fold of fat above his white collar, before glancing back to the door. "Well," he began, having more to say but wanting to show propriety. "Let's go inside and talk."

The front doorway that protruded from the building's main structure, led into a small waiting area just big enough for two. There was another door beyond the first, a little more than an arm span away. It was painted red and lined with wood, but with a solid core, buttressed with lead bolts. Much more secure than Dolly's cell at Falconwood, the red door to Harvey's Brig was an alert to all who saw it outside, a warning of where crime would lead you should you dare.

Ethel had heard that the Pownal Square jail was squalid, but as she entered into the main office that filled the entryway, the area seemed sparse and yet, cluttered at the same time.

Stairs led up to the second of three floors. Bits of debris and mud crowded the corners of each stair, and the paint was chipping from heavy boots climbing up and down each day. There was a billboard on the right wall, tacked with many different forms, flyers, and offenders on the run. At the back, Ethel saw a room set up almost like a small apartment. She guessed it to be the jailor's quarters.

"I'm just gonna come out and say that I don't approve of this one bit." Thomas Harvey shut the red door and led them into his office, left of the stairs. A window, lined with bars, looked out towards the soggy streets and an awaiting stagecoach. Besides the warden's desk and chair, there were chests, cabinets, and catalogue racks and drawers.

"This isn't any place for a lady," the jailor continued, sitting down in his creaking chair and fetching a cigar that had been smouldering in a nearby ashtray.

"Aren't there women incarcerated here?" Ethel asked, regarding an open chest that looked to be filled with soiled prison uniforms.

Mr. Harvey laughed around the thick cylinder of his cigar. "If they're here, they ain't ladies." He stood up and regarded

Constable Bertram. "He's already in the back, but this place isn't a hotel."

Ethel smiled, and whilst placing a hand on Andrew's shoulder, she spoke up on her own behalf. "Nor should it be, Mr. Harvey. Hard men beget hard homes. Thank you for your service to those who would see Charlottetown's criminals punished for their crimes. I appreciate it." Ethel smiled and watched as the jailor's face softened.

Mr. Harvey cleared his throat. "I understand your desire to see the man who killed your brother, Miss Arsenault, but confrontation will not cure your grief."

"No... but if I never stand before John Dowie and ask him why, I will always wonder and regret not doing so when I had a chance."

Thomas Harvey let out a breath through his nostrils, the ruminating noise as he considered her words a prelude to his stride across the floor.

"I've already told the constable, he could take you in as long as he accompanies you."

"And you've made your objections clear." Ethel nodded.

The door was at the right of the warden's office entrance. It was large, with six uniform holes bored above a brass knob. With a glance back at her, Harvey pulled it ajar, revealing a room void of light but for six lights at the very back.

It was some kind of holding cell or perhaps the room where prisoners were stripped of their clothes and belongings. A lone pole bisected the room, heavy with knicks and dents that seemed to have no effect on its sturdiness. Like spider eyes, the light from the opposite wall gleamed through another six holes in the facing door.

"This way," Harvey continued, heading forward into a lit room.

The visiting chamber was a stark area, covered in water damage and grime. On the walls were lit sconces, while the steel pipes of the gas line snaked in chaos on the ceiling. On the left side of the room, heavy brown bars secured two small cells adjoined via a table. It was built into the partitioning, steel-lined wall.

Mr. John Dowie sat on one side.

"He's already been secured," Andrew assured her as the jailor opened the visitor's cell where Ethel was to sit. He must have been led in via a door on the left-hand side of the room. Ethel guessed that beyond that door, there must have been a cluster of cells on the ground floor.

"Well, he's all yours, Miss. I'll be in my office?" Thomas Harvey waited until Constable Bertram nodded before walking away. Ethel stared into the visitor's cell, wondering if the barred door would lock behind her as she entered. The only thing on which to sit was a bench, whose paint was chipped and flaking.

Ethel studied the small details of the room until she was sure she could recall the space in her dreams.

As Andrew touched her elbow, Ethel started. "I'll wait right here," he said.

"All right." Before her legs had the chance to give out, Ethel entered the cell and sat down before him.

John Dowie was in uniform. The faded, horizontal black and white stripes were made into irregular box shapes from light pouring through the bars. He looked at her with tired eyes that suited his face and yet were much too old to belong to a man of his age.

His boyish youth was but a phantom haunting the tomb-like burrows of his face. The strength of his chin supported gaunt cheeks, while full lips crouched low like twin knolls over a calm lake. His hair was tousled above tired eyes, filled too early with demons, and the crest of his brow was downturned, causing chasms between his eyes and in the centre of his forehead.

He looked so young, and yet not. Though he couldn't have been but a year or two older than herself, Ethel was spooked by the dread upon his face, and the defeat.

I wanted a monster. Are you a monster, Mr. Dowie?

He returned her gaze with bleak surrender, but as Ethel stared, he did not look away. It was as though he expected her

259

to confront him and knew that he deserved it.

"God damn you, John Dowie," Ethel whispered, loud enough that the constable stirred in the corner. Ethel watched as her words struck him, and John Dowie's corpse-like nonchalance was transformed into shock.

Ethel leant in. Her eyes, like sharp instruments, were peeling the dermis back to see inside his mind. She saw regret, and she saw apology, and her hands began to shake. Ethel wanted to see his evil, his hate and his monstrosity.

Is that what I came for?

She held her head in her hands and rubbed at her temples with both thumbs.

Now that I'm here, I don't know what to say? What should I say? What should I do?

"Miss Eth—"

"Can you tell me why? Can you tell me what *happened*?"

Mr. Bertram, who had stood out of concern, sat down at a chair by the door.

Ethel continued, "I want to know what happened. I want you to tell me." She looked aside, and her body tensed as she cradled her shaking hands within her lap. "I promise you I will hate you no more for it."

Did she hate him? It seemed the proper thing, but Ethel didn't and was unsure why.

John Dowie leant back as he deflated from the shock of her language. He licked his lips and scratched at his chin, both eyes glassy yet proud.

"I was living in the house before you had even arrived," he looked back at her and frowned. "It wasn't my idea, but Dolly's. Was just gonna be for a few days until my ship was set to sail, but then... it started happening every time I came to port."

How did you meet Dolly? She wanted to ask but didn't wish to interrupt his story. He looked disturbed, like a dying man at the edge of an empty well, pulling a bucket of rocks up with his last few ounces of strength... hoping they would slake his thirst.

"Dolly and I were old friends. We grew up together. My mum used to work for hers, and we'd play in the stables a lot. Brush the horses and feed them." Regret peppered the lines around his mouth before he continued, "Look, I ain't a man that wants to explain himself to someone who was just a... an innocent bystander. You've done nothing but suffer from this, and I apologise for that." He sighed.

"From what I hear, your brother was a much better man than I—God knows that there was no sin of which I was not guilty." Dowie paused and blinked back the water that was welling at the corners of his eyes. "I *am* sorry, for what it's worth, and maybe that's all I've a right to be, but... can you tell Dolly—"

Andrew stirred. Dowie shook his head.

"Never mind. I suppose I should have said it myself before all this happened." He looked away, and yet, through the bars, Ethel could see him perfectly.

"Dolly loved my brother," Ethel said, arching her back until she sat ramrod with her chin tipped up. "She said so herself."

She wanted to hurt him, to leave him sitting in this squalid prison like a wounded beast, but as he regarded her, her body slackened at the effort it took to hate him.

"He was worthy of it. Wish I could say the same."

Ethel stood up, the scrape of the wooden bench signal enough for Andrew Bertram, who was at the cell door immediately. She didn't wait for him as she sped out of the visiting chamber, trying to match a speed that wouldn't give away her intention as she passed the warden's office. The outdoors was sickening as she departed the Pownal Street Jail, the red mud a gory sludge accompanied by the smell of brine. Ethel could hear Thomas Harvey's voice from inside, a curious blur of noise that followed her as she climbed into the stagecoach.

Why did I act like that? Why do I feel bad about it? What did I even hope to accomplish!

She beat her hands against her lap, her fruitless endeavours to breathe and calm down only igniting her ire.

Ethel screamed, not caring that the noise might carry, until she was finished screaming. By then, the cab door had reopened, and Andrew Bertram climbed aboard, his jacket still buttoned from the haste of his venture. He was holding her face in his hands, his eyes wild shields of worry.

"Miss Arsenault, please, it's all right! Shhh—I'm with you. Ethel, I'm with you!"

She didn't want to think. Thinking had led her here. To Dowie, to a reflection of herself that she didn't want to recognize.

With quivering lips, Ethel looked up at Andrew and gasped before kissing him. The ardent passion of her mouth, fuelled by the eagerness to escape all reason and thought, penetrated past propriety as she yanked at his collar, then pulled her hair free.

His lips were phantoms given flesh, first lost in the cold tomb of rectitude and modesty, and yet kindled by the eagerness of the woman before him.

Andrew pushed her back, and Ethel relished in the wake of his control. As his mouth began kissing down her neck, he braced himself with a knee on the bench beside her, pinning her in place and making her less accountable. His hands were upon her throat and were encouraging as she undid the ebony buttons of her mourning attire. Pale flesh that had never before seen sunlight was kissed by the darkness of the stagecoach, and as it lurched, Ethel closed her eyes. She pictured herself as Dolly, loving a man while Roland was away at sea.

Only he wasn't at sea... because Roland
had died a long time ago.

Chapter 25

"The trial had been a matter of days. With his own confession, Jonathan Dowie had sealed his fate and was sentenced to hang by the neck until dead. Appeals for clemency were made on his behalf but fell on deaf ears. John Dowie had killed an important man. Ernest Arsenault, a man committed to the development of Charlottetown, had been killed and made a cuckold of. Many residents of Charlottetown, by proxy, also felt like they'd been wronged.

Dolores Arsenault, Ernest's former wife, was unable to attend. It was decreed, despite her absence, that all of Ernest's assets would be reverted to his sister Ethel, in light of Dolly's adultery. Dolores Arsenault would not hang for any crimes."

Proclamation of Town Crier

* * *

It had been a week since Dowie's trial, and several days since Ethel first got word that Dolly was allowed to leave Falconwood. The rumours of Typhus were squashed by the news of the hanging. Many people of Charlottetown loathed the idea of such barbaric corporal punishments but found their voices lost in the face of such tragedy.

"Are you finished with that one, Beulah?" Ethel called from her room. "I don't want to leave anything behind. All else will be going to the estate sale." She peered at the bed, at the worn copy of Little Women, and her own journal. "I can't believe I haven't found a single photograph of him..."

The sun was strong and cast its shine across the floor in a brilliant curtain. There were only a few chests in here, packed with the scarce amount of belongings Ethel had thought to bring. A few portraits had been removed, and ornaments deemed important were wrapped and put away for transport. In the corner of most rooms were white sheets, draped over furniture deemed too cumbersome or unimportant to take.

"Everything is finished over there, Miss Ethel." Beulah was rubbing at her hands with a cloth. Her hair was tied up with a few added ribbons that she'd been gifted recently. "The only thing left is upstairs and... Ernest's office."

Ethel nodded. "Leave the office. There will be people coming to make sure it all goes where it's supposed to."

"Are you sure about all this, Miss Ethel? I don't mind accompanying you."

Ethel turned, and her shadow fell across Beulah. Ethel thought the woman looked lovely, and younger since they'd first arrived at Eden Hall.

"Fritz will be my escort. You need to stay, take care of things, live your life and come to know it." Ethel gripped her friend's biceps and squeezed, in part because she was happy, and because she knew she'd miss Beulah terribly. "Al is here... so I know he'll keep you out of trouble."

"Trouble?" Beulah laughed, kicking a fuss as she pulled away and meandered back towards the hall. "That's all that man knows! I'll be lucky if I'm back by next summer with all the *trouble* he's bound to unearth."

Ethel chuckled, glad for Beulah's mirth. She would miss her terribly when she left Eden Hall, and yet, even Beulah couldn't make Ethel stay.

"I know I've said this before, Miss Ethel, and I'll only bother you about it once more, but... shouldn't you visit Dolly? At least once before you leave?"

Ethel offered a sad smile, her eyes drawing from Beulah towards the floor.

"I don't... know," she said, moving towards the bed to take a seat as Beulah joined her. Her eyes stared ahead, towards the door, unfocused as she built the scales of pro et contra in her mind. "After speaking with Mr. Dowie, I—I didn't want to at all. In my mind, Dolly helped to murder my brother." Ethel cocked her head to the side.

"What could Dolly ever say that could change my mind? *That's* what I thought, and still think now."

Beulah exhaled through her nose, her words of comfort: wind against a rock wall. Not knowing what to say, she took and held on to Ethel's arm.

"You don't have to, Miss Ethel, but if you don't, you could regret it."

"I wonder if regret is stronger than spite and anger?"

Beulah shook her head. "Maybe not, Miss Ethel, but are you certain you want all three?"

Ethel frowned and leant in against her.

Jonathan Dowie was set to hang, and though Dolly had been proven innocent, she hadn't been able to leave Falconwood until the quarantine was lifted. It had been so several days ago, and yet Ethel had refused to let Al go fetch her.

After I leave, you may go. But I've no wish to see her. Not now or ever again.

Had Ethel changed her mind?

"I'm sorry, Miss—"

"No. Don't be." Ethel shook her head, interrupting with a reassuring pat. "You're right. I—despite it all, I need to see her before I go. I'll leave no ghosts behind this time..." Ethel stood and took Miss Murphy with her. "Thank you, Beulah," she said, pulling the woman in for a warm embrace. "You will be more than enough reason for me to come back here."

"It's a lovely city, really," Beulah replied, sniffing to hold back tears.

"All the more lovelier with you in it." Ethel pulled away and waved a hand in front of her face to keep herself from crying. "All right now, no more of this. If I have to go to Falconwood, I'll do it without having cried once already."

The two women laughed and righted their attire as the sun shined in luminous ribbons.

"I'll tell Al to get the carriage ready." Beulah paused on her way to the door, as though a thought had just occurred to her. "Do you wish for me to come with you, Miss Ethel?"

Ethel's smile grew, a hint of appreciation softening her features. "No, that's all right Beulah. A quiet ride there and a quiet ride back, will clear my mind."

"Well... I can be quiet, you know?"

Ethel chuckled, louder this time. "Not with Al Carlow driving the coach!"

Beulah made a face, sticking out her tongue like they used to do as kids.

As Beulah left the room, Ethel sighed and pivoted on her heel to take in the entire bedchamber. She wondered when they were planning Eden Hall, who they intended this room for. What did her brother have in mind when it was first designed?

It doesn't matter now.

She was set to leave in a week or two. She both dreaded and looked forward to it.

* * *

Ethel had enough time to wash up, pack her Gladstone, and find her shawl before Al came to fetch her. It was a ride she was well used to by now, and yet, as the wheels conformed to the dry ruts of the road, she found it bumpy and the stagecoach cramped. The day was unseasonably warm for April, and her high-necked, black dress was like a heavy wool around her. Ethel dabbed at her chin with a handkerchief, wondering if this was Ernest telling her to go back, that this was folly.

He wouldn't say that. Not Ernie. Like Beulah, he would want me to go. To look at her in his place and ask why.

The main hall inside the asylum was a chasm compared to the first time Ethel had arrived. The audience of residents, clustered for a photograph, was replaced with trolleys and polished floors. The doors to each room were all shut, though a nurse was at the front, sitting at a desk that hadn't been there before.

"Hello." Ethel removed her gloves and glanced towards the hall. "I am here to see Dolores Arsenault."

"Oh! Miss Arsenault." The nurse looked up and patted her skirts as she stood up from the desk and walked around it to meet her. "Thank you for coming."

Ethel recognized her. "You're the photographer," *who had paled when I had first come to see Dolly.*

"I am. Nurse Grubb." Her sunny enthusiasm faded, though Ethel could see the woman was taking pains to hide it. "It's so nice to see you again. I-I must apologise for everything, Miss Arsenault. We had a Typhus outbreak before and it—"

Ethel nodded and tried to stop the worms in her belly from squirming. "I understand, Nurse Grubb. How is she doing?" Ethel frowned, catching the panic in the woman's eye as she began to lead her out from the entryway.

"It's—well," the nurse stumbled. "I mean, she's doing as well as expected. It may be better to hear it from her, though."

Why? Her interest was charged with worry and doubt, made more so as they continued down the same route they'd first taken weeks ago.

"Dolly's still down in the cellars? But she's not being watched anymore, is she?"

The nurse flashed her an anxious glance before looking away.

Ethel thought perhaps Nurse Grubb intended to pretend she hadn't heard her, but after a moment of walking, she spoke up.

"No. All the officers have gone, but... it's more comfortable for her down there, c-considering all her belongings."

There was a pang of guilt that speared Ethel's breast.

I should have sent someone to get her. I should have come sooner...

The door to the room was closed, though the lock had been dismantled. Dolly could come and go as she pleased, and that was a small comfort.

"She's inside. I—" the nurse hesitated, backing away towards where they had just come. "I need to attend to the other residents. Is there anything more you need, Miss Arsenault?"

Ethel shook her head and watched the woman leave. She wondered if all the staff of Falconwood were anxious, and if it were due to the trial and eventual hanging of John Dowie.

Looking askance towards the door, Ethel pursed her lips. A wave of trepidation was stiffening her muscles.

Why am I here? To confront her? To say goodbye?

No. What Ethel really wanted was to see if Dolly was all right, and to see, after the fact, if the last several days had changed her.

Ethel opened the door, and like last time, stepped across the large threshold. The heat of the afternoon didn't penetrate the cellar as it did the upper floors and was a small mercy to those confined here. She could hear a woman yelling from somewhere, but the voice was faint, blocked by the heavy stone walls.

Dolly looked up from the bed as Ethel entered, her hair undone and limp around her shoulders. Her face was pale, and though the curtains were open to let in sunlight, the rays did not penetrate as far as the bed.

She was wearing a shift, and her legs, thrown over the side of the bed as she sat, were bare. A sheen of perspiration made her face look like the belly of a clam, and a bucket at her bedside gave the impression that she had been ill for a few days.

"Dolly?" Ethel called, her anger and spite melting before the sickly face of her sister-in-law. Dolly looked more like a resident of Falconwood than she had the first time Ethel had visited.

"Etty..." Her eyes were tired and red, and dark bruise-like bags hung beneath them. She was holding her belly as though she may retch, and Ethel had to keep herself from going to fetch the bucket for her.

"Dolly, I—What happened to you?" The rumours of Typhus had been squashed. Falconwood had opened under the pretence that there was no risk of contagion. Was this a result of the news? Of Dowie's hanging and prosecution?

"Ethel I... I am so glad you've come. I worried that you'd leave without seeing me."

Another spasm of guilt wracked her brain, and despite all that had happened, Ethel couldn't help but wish she had come right away.

"I'm sorry, Dolly."

Dolly held up a hand. "No," she replied, her breathing laboured. "I am the one who is sorry. If I am in such a pitiful state, it is of my own doing." She groaned as she attempted to stand. The shift floated around her body, and Ethel saw how much thinner Dolly was now.

"I found this in some of the chests that were brought out to me. I wanted you to have it."

It was sealed within an envelope, and as Dolly tore the paper open, Ethel saw her own name scribbled on the front.

She must have meant to send it out. Dolly didn't think I'd come...

It was a photograph of Ernest. He was younger, thinner, his face regal and serious. It must have been from before the two were married, but only just, as it had a line written on the back.

"With love, from Ernie," Ethel read, tears streaming down her face. She couldn't keep her emotions in as she clutched at the photograph and thought of her journal.

I'll never forget his face now.

"I know you think I'm a monster, Etty. That I used your brother and betrayed him." Dolly avoided her gaze. Her hand was resting on the back of the chair for support, and she groaned as though something unseen was causing her pain. "But, despite all that, I never wanted to see him hurt... I never wanted—" she buckled over, knees crashing to the floor as she clutched at her midsection. Ethel started, eyes wide and worried. Setting the picture on the desk, Ethel crouched to look at her and hovered her hands about Dolly's shoulders, unsure as to whether she ought to reach out.

"I loved them both, Etty. I loved them both! They were both chambers in my damned, foolish heart." Dolly squeezed her eyes shut, a shock of pain crumpling her in half before she could speak again.

"Dolly, what—"

"I never meant for any of this to happen, Etty. I didn't mean for Ernest to die. I was a stupid girl who scorned the home Ernest had so lovingly built." She sat up a little. Her eyes stared ahead as though phantoms were dancing in the beading tears falling in streams down her cheeks. "Now John is going to hang because I couldn't give anything up. I had to have it all!"

Ethel sat back, disgust and worry enveloping her features.

"I was lonely."

Loneliness.

Ethel understood loneliness.

Loneliness was being called *Miss* Arsenault, even though she'd been engaged and married to Roland in her heart. Loneliness was drawing those you missed in a journal. Loneliness was a black dress. Everyday. Until your normal clothes no longer fit you.

"You think I've never been lonely?" Ethel said, her fists hammers in her lap. "Or is it that you know I'll understand? Poor Dolly, she was *lonely*. So much so that her husband called his sister out to keep her company." She yelled, "You had *everything*, and you threw it all away! You had Dowie in the house, even when I was there. You poisoned me! You made me think the house was haunted! You *asked* me to lie and say it was a ghost."

Ethel turned her head away and stared at the exit, unlocked beyond the threshold. She thought of leaving, of locking the door and never coming back, but as Dolly cried and crawled away, Ethel watched as she retched into the bucket.

"Dolly—"

She did it again and again, until she was dry heaving from an empty stomach.

Ethel collected a glass of water by the bedside and proffered it to her. "Dolly, what is—"

"I'm pregnant, Ethel," she said between gasps. "I'm pregnant. They thought I was afflicted with some horrible contagion, but all it is is..."

"Pregnant?" Ethel sat back along the floor. The cool press of stone beneath her palms felt like fire. "Pregnant," she said again, touching her belly. "Dolly, for how long?"

Dolly took a drink, spat it out into the bucket and took another. "Several weeks, at least. The doctor said I was not far along, and that's the reason for my sickness." She closed her eyes and shook her head, and as though expecting the question, said, "I don't know who the father is."

Ethel was lost. Memories of Roland crashed to the surface. Stale hopes, seasoned with her brother's death.

Auntie Etty...

Ethel covered her mouth to keep herself from sobbing. "Are you sure, Dolly?"

She nodded. "I am. I wasn't going to tell you, even in that letter." Dolly looked up towards the envelope that had contained the photo. A small, folded paper had been tossed beneath it. "But now that you're here—"

"How could you consider not telling me?" Ethel cried, her bottom lip quivering.

"Because I didn't know if it was Ernest's! Because I didn't want you to hope that it was, when we will never, *ever* know for sure!"

Her heart was rending in two, and yet, as Ethel wept upon the floor, she glanced at Dolly's belly and saw the subtle bump of impending motherhood.

What should I do?

Ethel tore at her hair and squeezed her eyes shut.

Auntie Etty! I wanted to be Auntie Etty... but Dolly—she killed Ernest. Shot him! What if the baby isn't an Arsenault at all? What if the baby's a...

"Dowie's been sentenced to hang. Dolly, what do you plan to do?"

"I don't know." She pushed the bucket away and drug her knees up to her chest to hold them. "I've thought about it over and over. One of the nurses suggested... but I can't. What if it was Ernest's? What if it was John's? This child would be my only reminder of them."

She looked up. "Ethel, I *loved* your brother! I loved him more than anything, but... John and I grew up together. He worked on the farm, was a stable boy for my father. He was my first kiss, my first little love affair, and when I saw him again, I—all my loneliness faded for a while.

"I loved Ernest so much, but he was always gone. My family and friends were all back home. I tried to make friends here, but I never really fit in. I wasn't born to wealth, Ethel, and when Ernest's business took off, all of a sudden, he was gone all the time."

"Why did you never tell him you were lonely? He would have understood."

Dolly shook her head, and a few loose strands stuck to the side of her face. "I didn't want to hurt him. He had built an entire paradise for me at Eden Hall. How could I tell him it felt more like a cage?"

"So, you killed him?" The words were like a gun blast from Ethel's mouth, and even though it hurt to say them, Ethel was relieved when Dolly recoiled.

"No. It was all an accident. A terrible accident." She inhaled.

"Ernest came home and found us together. I think he thought Johnathan was a burglar. Ernest had the gun on him, but as the two fought, Ernest was the one who was shot. Ethel, Johnathan was the one who spiked your drink. He thought Ernest had already left, and he wanted, well... a night together. He got a kick out of terrorising you, and I... didn't stop him."

Dolly regarded her, and though she seemed like she was trying to hold herself together, anguish shattered her features. She set her head down and banged her forehead on her knees.

"He said it was all in good fun, that he was having a hard time sneaking out, and that staying in the attic all day was lonesome."

"Why the attic? How could there have been no other place for him to stay?"

"I'm sure there was, but I was... daft. John was a sailor. If he wasn't sailing, then there wasn't much money. I gave him a few pieces of jewellery to sell, but I foolishly rationed that if he just stayed in the attic, then he didn't have to spend anything." Dolly gave a dry chuckle. "Of course, then, anytime I was alone or depressed, he was there. It was mutually beneficial." Ethel frowned, and catching it, Dolly sighed.

"This is all so selfish of me, I know. But, when I first saw John after so many years, it... it wasn't like a surge of emotions had overwhelmed my senses. It was more a subtle curiosity. I had been in town with Adella, and he had come in with the other sailors. We had a drink, reminisced a bit, and went our separate ways." Dolly chewed at her inner cheek. "It wasn't some re-lived romance. I didn't feel *anything* for him that day except curious."

How could that be true?

"Except I kept seeing him, running into him. And when the occasional coincidence became more than was deemed appropriate, I'd make excuses.

I wanted a friend. I wanted someone I didn't need to spend time getting to know in order to open myself up to them. John was... already half there, and the more we saw of each other, the more the feelings changed.

"I spent... so much time with him, Ethel. And even when I had realised that I crossed the line, I didn't want to give either one up, because I loved them both.

"On occasion, John *did* go off to sea. When Ernest was scheduled to be home, or when John had debts to pay, he'd leave for a while."

"He came back the night we went to the Windmill, right?"

Dolly nodded. "I'm sorry, Ethel. I didn't know you were set to arrive here so early." She smiled. "I think Ernest meant for you to be somewhat of a gift."

From Ernest. Because of course, you'd try and surprise your wife.

Ethel wiped at her eyes, though a small smile graced her lips.

Dolly continued, "I thought maybe I could have them both, both Johnny and Ernest, but... I was being selfish and cruel, and now…" she began to cry anew, "and now Ernie is *dead* and John's to be hanged and the only memory I have of them both is this child, who will never know who their father really is!"

Ethel crawled forward, her beating heart pounding past the pain and hurt of Dolly's words. She was sobbing for Dolly, her heart twisting in pain at the anguish pouring from Dolly's chest. Ethel took her in her arms, and the both of them rocked back and forth, crying and clinging to one another.

"It doesn't matter. Dolly, it… doesn't matter. The child will be an Arsenault because *you* are an Arsenault, and *I* am your sister."

"Ethel—"

"I won't abandon you, Dolly," Ethel said, cradling Dolly's head beneath her chin. "I may not forgive you right away, but I won't leave you here alone. You can come to Summerside with me. We will harvest potatoes and catch fireflies and raise this child to know where his father came from."

"But—"

Ethel shushed her. "You're not an evil woman, Dolly. I don't believe you meant ill, even though your actions were selfish and self-serving. And—" Ethel stared ahead, her thoughts unfocusing her eyes. "I've lost enough people in my life. I understand. And whether or not you were selfish or cruel, I do believe you loved those men." *Both of them, who were fated to die.*

Could I stop it? Should I? Do I want to?

No... but I can be here when it happens for you. And for the pain that it causes, I will forgive you, because we both have suffered much too much for the length of time we've been alive.

Ethel kissed the crown of Dolly's head, and the girl shivered.

"Let's get you back to Eden Hall," she said, helping Dolly to her feet.

"Thank you, Etty."

Ethel wiped her eyes and nodded as Dolly embraced her. She could feel the press of Dolly's stomach squeeze against her own, and the warmth therein delighted her.

"You're welcome," Ethel said. *A small thanks, for making me Auntie Etty.*

Chapter 26

"It already doesn't fit me."

The three women were peering into a mirror on the third story of Eden Hall. Dolly was in the front, a long black gown falling around her figure like an hourglass. Behind her, Ethel was making sure that each small button in the train along Dolly's back was fastened in the correct way.

Beulah was fussing with her hair, jutting every available pin she could find off Dolly's vanity into her head to keep it from falling out of place.

Ethel was trying not to chuckle at Dolly. "The dress will fit for today at least. Though you *are* beginning to show."

Dolly looked down at her belly and splayed both hands overtop like a shell. She was still small, and her stomach had been easily camouflaged, but the starkness of Dolly's white hands over her black tummy gave the impression of an empty ribcage spanning across her stomach.

"I know you're not all right. Do you want to talk about it, Dolly?" Ethel asked, glancing over at Beulah who had quit her grumbling in the face of solemnity.

Dolly shrugged, but there was emotion sparkling in her eyes. "No. Talking about it won't change anything and besides, you both wouldn't understand." She looked sidelong, and as bleak comprehension struck, Dolly smiled.

Beulah and I are attending the hanging of a man who killed our friend and brother.

You're attending a loved one's funeral.

Ethel nodded.

"I have something for you," she said, fetching a box from her Gladstone. The windows were open to let in the sunlight, and a bird alighted on the windowsill. "I meant to give this to you earlier, but... here."

The box was velvet with a silver trim. It was clasped with a pewter hook.

"Are they...swallows?" Dolly asked, holding the box aloft in one hand.

"Yes, and they're good luck." She took one of the two matching birds perched upon a silk cloth and pinned it upon Dolly's breast. "Swallows have a connection to the sea, and they symbolise love and patience." Ethel took the other and pinned it at the hollow of her own neck. "Lazuli is a stone of truth."

You may wear yours for John if you like. But I will wear mine for Ernest.

"T-thank you, Etty. I—" Dolly watched her reflection in the mirror and turned the pin from side to side to see how it caught the light. "I..." she was breaking down, reliving a future that had not yet passed.

Ethel embraced her. They had told her not to go, but Dolly had insisted. She had to see him one last time and look at him so he knew she was all right, that she still loved him.

Dolly hadn't said so, but Ethel knew, and so they all resolved to go together.

"Have you been reading Little Women?" Ethel asked as Dolly settled. The small novel had been on the desk when Ethel entered, but she had yet to enquire about it.

Dolly sniffed and wiped her cheek. "I've actually finished it already," she said, her eyes softening. "Falconwood gave me plenty of time to read, and I saw you reading it once. One of the nurses was kind enough to bring it to me."

Ethel was touched. "Did you like it? I've read it through a few times. I think I'm on chapter forty now."

"I did—"

"If you're takin' Dolly back to Summerside, I'm afraid you'll never read again, Miss Ethel." Beulah stifled a laugh and sat down upon the nearby window box.

"What does that mean, Beulah?" Dolly replied, staring daggers at the young maid. Beulah giggled.

Ethel leant over Dolly's shoulder and whispered in her ear, "I think it means *you* talk almost as much as *she* does." Ethel laughed, flinching away from Beulah's physical retort.

Chapter 27

Dear Diary,

It is the seventh day of April, in the year of 1869. We are on our way to Summerside. The day is rife with the cawing of gulls and the whisper of the conspiring sea. Dolly sits beside me on deck, a woollen shawl around her shoulders. The paddlewheel of the Princess of Wales is loud, but Dolly hasn't had an inclination to talk since yesterday, so it's a welcome excuse for silence.

Beulah and Al had seen us off at the dock, promising to write and keep Eden Hall in tip top shape. I already miss her, dear Beulah, who I can't remember ever being without. I feel a bit like I expect a new mother may feel, leaving the safety of one I care about, to help another in need. But Dolly needs me, more than ever, and in a way, I need her to.

"Ethel?"

Ethel looked over, and the coast of Prince Edward Island lay like a platter atop the cerulean sea. Dolly looked up at her.

"Yes, Dolly?"

Her eyes were sallow, and huddled in her shawl she looked twice the age she'd been when Ethel had first arrived at Charlottetown.

"What about the Constable? What about Mr. Bertram?"

Ethel sighed and pulled the woman beneath her arm.

Ethel was tired of love affairs, of romance and passion, but... she wondered if Beulah had told Dolly of Andrew. "I'm not sure, Dolly. I hope we meet again someday, when we're all of us in a better place, but—"

He had wanted to come with her, escort her to Summerside. But after yesterday he'd decided to stay and promised to write when he could.

It was better that way. Bertram was like the sequel to a story she really wanted to read but knew she'd never have any time for. Ethel's life was in shambles, and Dolly needed time to heal. She hoped she saw the constable again, in his dusty suit. She hoped she could meet him in a pretty dress. Not black, but green, and with flowers...

"Don't worry about him, dear," Ethel said, kissing the crown of her head as Dolly leant towards her.

Ethel opened her diary and read back the last sentence. Dolly closed her eyes.

The papers are already calling it the last hanging on the island. Poor John Dowie, not even he deserved the fate he got. That Dolly was there, watching him till the very end...

Ethel looked out at the sea and thought of Roland.

She glanced back down at the diary.

A rough sketch of a man was on the page before. He had a strong chin above gaunt cheeks, and full lips crouched low like twin knolls over a calm lake. His boyish youth, quashed beneath eyes filled with demons, was collared with a noose.

Next to his picture was another entry.

Diary,

I've only just returned home and got Dolly into bed. The whole of Charlottetown is in anarchy after the hanging of one unfortunate man: John Dowie. Even I, a victim of his heinous crimes, bear woe for a man hung twice. How terrible it must have been to wake within the prison cell after making peace with death, to learn again that you must hang by the neck till dead.

Sixteen feet he fell. At the conclusion of his poem—addressed to mother and wife— he stood atop the gallows and fell quiet as the platform sprung. He had spoken for a half hour and admitted to his crimes. I'll remember his words always, like a ghost in the halls of my mind.

"Although my hand has done the deed for which I am to die, I never for an instant thought, to cause such horrid strife. Nor would I, for ten thousand worlds, take a fellow creature's life."

Fifteen hundred people had gathered to watch him die, and with such inflated numbers, the military was called. Men with bayonets. Sixty of them. In attendance.

When the trap was sprung, the rope broke, and Dowie fell sixteen feet. The roar of spectators was deafening. A Mad chorus—some aligned with those who thought hanging barbaric and cruel, and then those cheering for his death—rose up amongst the crowd. When John Dowie rose to his knees, the crowd surged and faced the assemblage of fixed bayonets.

Stunned! He had been stunned, but imagine waking as the crowd outside roared, and the jailor began tying another noose around your neck!

Diary... I rue wishing for the death of a man. Dolly, in my arms, wept, and I saw wild hope within her eyes.

Clemency! Clemency! The crowd commands. Hope slides deep within the belly of the fifteen hundred, pumping most fiercely in the heart of Dolores Arsenault.

But as the hour passed, and Dowie returned to the gallows, again he hung and fell to the ground.

How could God be on your side, John Dowie, when it left the side of my brother?

I thought that then, but I regret it
now.

The newspapers say it was out of sympathy that they hauled him up, eight feet above the ground. Out of sympathy they fought the crowd for forty minutes as Dowie hanged and died.

What have I become to wish a fate so foul on another human being? The sight of a fellow mortal, being thus so inhumanly launched into eternity, will haunt me for my life, and I can only hope, Dolly's mind, and the mind of the child, be saved from the horror of that man's slaying.

"Ethel?"

"Yes?" She closed her book and looked down into Dolly's beautiful blue eyes.

"Why did you agree to take the boats back? Are you not scared of them?"

Ethel paused and looked over the sapphire sea laced with foam and seaweed. "Did you love Dowie, Dolly?"

Ethel caught the surprise in her sister's features and the shameful blush of red that peppered her alabaster cheeks like the bloom of poppies. "I did, yes."

"Well," Ethel held her close and sat back against the ship's bench as she stared above the guardrail. "If you can watch the man you love hang twice, I can ride a boat. Ernest was always saying I ought to."

At her side, Dolly was weeping, and the sound of the paddlewheel carried on filling the silence between them.

Ethel looked down at the swallow on her breast pocket, and then the one adorning Dolly's.

And they were no longer little girls, but little women, and they lived...

Ethel wiped her eyes. *Well... they lived,* she thought. *At least...*

Together we will try.

The End

Vanessa wrote her first story when she was in grade five. It was entitled *Mutilated* and warranted a trip to the school guidance counsellor. With over a dozen publications under her belt, Twice Hung serves as her first voyage into Historical Fiction and Mystery. Vanessa has won numerous awards for her books and she's conducted workshops all over New Brunswick. In her spare time, she dabbles in paint and acrylics.

Vanessa C. Hawkins books also published by BWL Publishing

The Curious Case of Simon Todd
Ballroom Riot
Bunker Blitz